Beware Taurus

Jo Hughes, astrologer and part time private investigator, has now recovered from her last dramatic murder case. She is just spending a quiet moment snooping in her boss's office when a well-dressed young man walks in. Little does Jo know that she's about to come face to face with danger and deception.

The man gives his name as Connor Fitzpatrick and tells Jo that he wants help looking for his brother Sean, who has been missing for over a week. Last Friday Sean went to the office as usual but he didn't turn up at work on Monday and Connor discovered that he'd booked Friday off. The last trace there is of him is a cash withdrawal made in Coventry. But the brothers live in London.

Jo is intrigued. Why would someone simply up and go like that? Was Sean Fitzpatrick running away from something – or someone? And what had prompted him to leave on that particular morning? Impulsively, Jo takes on the case, knowing she's going to enjoy finding out more about Sean's disappearance – and about the handsome Connor, come to that.

In search of clues, Jo resolves to cast Sean's horoscope. But even the grim predictions for Taureans that week couldn't have forewarned her of the fate of the missing man. And Jo's own horoscope (for Virgos) predicts turbulent times ahead...

By the same author:

BLOOD OF AN ARIES

Beware Taurus

Linda Mather

MACMILLAN
LONDON

First published 1994 by Macmillan London Limited

a division of Pan Macmillan Publishers Limited
Cavaye Place London SW10 9PG
and Basingstoke

Associated companies throughout the world

ISBN 0-333-62070-4

Copyright © Linda Mather 1994

The right of Linda Mather to be identified as the
author of this work has been asserted by her in accordance
with the Copyright, Designs and Patents Act 1988.

All rights reserved. No reproduction, copy or transmission
of this publication may be made without written permission.
No paragraph of this publication may be reproduced, copied or
transmitted save with written permission or in accordance with
the provisions of the Copyright Act 1956 (as amended). Any
person who does any unauthorised act in relation to
this publication may be liable to criminal prosecution
and civil claims for damages.

9 8 7 6 5 4 3 2 1

A CIP catalogue record for this book is available from
the British Library

Typeset by Intype, London
Printed by Mackays of Chatham PLC, Chatham, Kent

To Wendy

Predictions for the week beginning 14th June:

TAURUS (April 22nd–May 21st)

You may find yourself on the horns of a dilemma this week – even facing some danger, so beware! Take a step back and try not to be too absorbed in your own plans. A friend or colleague might just be leading you by the ring in your nose so watch out – people close to you can be unpredictable at times. Now is a good time to start planning a long break away from it all but don't rush into things. Saturn is moving into retrograde this week which could mean a downturn in fortunes both emotional and financial, so try and devote some time to any worries before things get out of hand. Play safe this week and don't take any unnecessary risks. Above all, beware of rash decisions!

Chapter One

'I'm going to lunch, Jo. Do you want anything?' Celia popped her head round the door, freshly lipsticked and beaming underneath a frosting of white, curly hair.

Jo covered the mouthpiece of the phone. 'Have we got enough coffee?'

'Plenty, but I'll get some more. Some of that vile Continental blend you like—'

'Not decaffeinated,' Jo called as Celia's head disappeared. In her ear she heard the administrative clerk in Dudley Road Hospital returning to the phone.

He came back full of apologies for keeping her waiting and confirmed that a certain Lee Kwok had worked at the hospital as a general nurse between 1982 and 1988, which was just the information Jo was looking for. She thanked him and flicked through the copy of Lee Kwok's application form. Yes, Ms Kwok had been telling the truth. Next to check her date of birth: Lee Kwok was a Capricorn, which meant she passed Jo's own private selection procedure and her completed form went on the left-hand pile.

This was one of the better jobs Jo had been given since she had started work at Macy and Wilson's Investigation Agency. A private hospital was opening up in Coventry and the new director had asked her boss, David Macy, to verify the references of short-listed applicants. Macy had passed the job on to Jo and she had added her own twist to the process. She was putting aside the forms of applicants born under Virgo and Capricorn and was intending to advise the director that these people would make the best nurses – according to astrological wisdom, anyway.

Jo picked up the last form and looked at it without enthusiasm. She had been doing the same job all morning and was finding it difficult to concentrate. She could hear Celia's high heels clattering down the stairs to the front door. It was very warm – summer had arrived unexpectedly – and the office was stuffy. This dark, poky room doubled up as a kitchen for the few staff at the agency and had one small window. Restless, Jo got up to look out, peering down at the backs of shops in the alley below.

Working as a part-time PI may have its tedious moments but Jo found she was surprisingly good at it. She had a certain amount of audacity combined with dogged perseverance. Anyway, she could put up with the more boring days because, she reminded herself, it was only temporary work until she could become a full-time astrologer. Her real passion was casting charts for people. Payment for this plus her weekly horoscope column for a local paper and wages from Macy meant she had just enough to live on. But even with the two jobs, her landlord still had to wait a couple of weeks for the rent now and again. And her mother moaned that she would never 'settle down with a mortgage'.

Jo turned back to the unfinished application form on her desk but it still did not appeal and she wandered out looking for coffee. There was none brewing in the reception area where Celia worked so Jo looked around for something else to divert her. It was unusual for her to have the whole place to herself. According to Celia, Macy had gone to Sheffield for the day and Jo, trying the door to his office, found it open. She had half expected it to be locked, knowing how jealously he guarded his privacy.

The cluttered, dusty room was not much better than the one she had just left. She opened both windows, sat in Macy's old, comfortable office chair and looked at the papers spread out on the desk. Neither they nor the room revealed much about Macy except he wasn't very tidy and didn't spend any money on office furniture. She knew remarkably little about him and, irritatingly, this made him more attractive.

Swivelling round in her chair, she looked at the filing cabinets behind her. They were unlabelled and probably full of more work files. She tried a few drawers and discovered she was right. But in the cabinet closest to the door she turned up a folder which contained some letters signed by Mark Wilson. Though the agency was called Macy and Wilson, no one had ever mentioned who Wilson was. Even Celia couldn't be drawn on the subject.

So he did exist then, Jo thought to herself. These letters were six years old, and looking back further in the file, she found one from an accountant, which listed three partners of Macy and Wilson: Mark Wilson, David Macy and Jill Macy. Now who was that – his sister or, more likely, his wife? He lived on his own in the flat above the office so he must be divorced now, Jo thought to herself, but why all the secrecy?

While she was delving into another file, Jo heard someone moving about in the outer office. Guiltily, realizing how she would hate to have her privacy invaded, she put the file back together and tried to peer through the frosted glass door. Theoretically clients could drop in to the agency but this did not often happen and it was unlike Celia to forget an appointment. Jo could see someone standing in the other room and hoped it wasn't Macy. Before she could get the filing cabinet closed, there was a gentle tap on the glass.

'Come in,' Jo called, and a man walked in, looking around with an air of hopeful enquiry. He was young, blond, smart and slightly flushed from the heat.

'Miss Macy or Miss Wilson?' He gave her a smile and held out his hand.

'Neither,' Jo explained, closing the filing cabinet

smoothly, 'I'm Jo Hughes. Mr Macy is out on business today. And Mr Wilson has – er – left the firm.' She took his proffered hand and he gave hers a single practised shake across the desk. There didn't seem much point in explaining that she had only borrowed the office so she offered him one of the battered old wooden chairs Macy kept for clients.

'Connor Fitzpatrick,' he said and handed her a business card. His narrow blue eyes flickered around the room from under a slightly disarrayed fringe, taking in the ordered clutter of Macy's office. 'I've never actually been to a private investigation agency before,' he said disarmingly.

'How can we help, Mr Fitzpatrick?' Jo asked, trying to observe the visitor discreetly. His card didn't tell her much. It was from a London firm of stockbrokers, about which she knew nothing.

He took a breath and leant forward, placing his palms together. 'We-ell, do you look for missing people? Because my brother has gone missing and it's difficult to get the police to take it seriously.'

'How long has he been gone?' Jo asked. She had been thinking how attractive Fitzpatrick was but now firmly redirected her thoughts.

'Nearly two weeks.' Fitzpatrick gave Jo a look that tried to anticipate her reaction. 'I suppose you think that's not long and I'm being a bit over-protective?'

She shook her head. 'Have you thought he might have been in an accident?' she asked, as delicately as she could.

'The police said that too but I've rung round all the hospitals. Thank God, he's not there.' Fitzpatrick paused, looking exasperated. 'The police advised me to give it a month and go back to them if I still hadn't heard from him. But I know something's wrong—'

'If you could tell me a bit more about his disappearance...?'

'All right,' he agreed. Fitzpatrick's self-assurance was obvious. He gave himself as much time as he wanted to collect his thoughts. Then he began speaking matter of factly again. 'Sean is thirty-three – that's four years older than me. He works for a bank and he's doing reasonably well at it. But he's very bright and could probably do a lot better if he wanted to. We share a house in Putney – we bought it two years ago – and although we don't exactly live in each other's pockets, I usually know roughly where he is.'

'Go on.'

'OK – a week last Friday he went off to the office as usual. I saw him at breakfast. We didn't say much but we never do at that time of day. We're both owls not larks, if you know what I mean. He seemed just the same as ever. He took a small holdall with him but I thought that was sports stuff. Went off in his car as if he was going to work. I found out later he'd booked that day off work but he didn't turn up when he was supposed to on the Monday. Now, ten days later, there's been no word from him – not a postcard. Not a phone call.' After Fitzpatrick had presented these facts, he sat back and waited for Jo's reaction.

She had been scribbling down some of this in a notepad she found on Macy's desk. 'We do take on cases like this,' she said with more confidence than she felt. 'We would bill you for our time, which is twenty-five pounds an hour plus expenses. I'd need to know a bit more – like where exactly your brother works?'

'At the National Commercial Bank in London. Do you know London very well?'

Jo paused in her note-taking and looked up. 'Yes, a bit – but if Sean lives and works in London, what are you doing in Coventry?'

'Well, I've started to do my own detective work.' He gave Jo a brief boyish smile. 'I know Sean came here on the eighteenth of June because I opened his last bank statement and he made a cash withdrawal from a bank in Coventry.'

'Do you know what he was doing here?'

Fitzpatrick shook his head. 'Maybe something to do with a woman – I've noticed a new voice on the answering machine lately.'

'A girlfriend?' Jo felt like she was building up a picture of Sean using baby's building blocks. But it was a start.

'Probably. He hasn't had a regular—' Fitzpatrick paused over the word – 'relationship for a while. But I think he was seeing someone new called Rosie. Knowing Sean, it wouldn't be anything serious.'

'Do you know how to get in touch with her?' Jo asked. When Fitzpatrick shook his head, she added, 'You said her voice is on the answering machine. Have you still got the tape?'

'No, I wiped it straight away. I always do. His car is still missing as well, by the way. I should have mentioned that.' He gave the make and registration and Jo scribbled this down along with the other notes she had been taking. This case appealed to her. It was fascinating to think that someone could just write themselves out of their own lives. It looked to her as if that's exactly what Fitzpatrick's brother had done.

'Has he been depressed lately?'

'No – he's not a moody person. He's been his usual easy-going self.'

'Do you know what he took with him?'

'I've looked in his room and it's difficult to say. All his clothes seem to be there. I found his passport, so he didn't take that. He had his credit cards, wallet, chequebook on him and I think he took some overnight stuff – his shaver was missing.'

'Have you thought he might not want to be found?' Jo asked tentatively. 'People do just decide to take off, don't they?'

Fitzpatrick shook his head soberly. 'It's possible but

even if he has, I want to know where he is.' He didn't expand on this but his mind was clearly made up and Jo knew Macy would not want her to talk a client out of employing them.

'All right, then. We'll see what we can do,' Jo heard herself say. Thinking of Macy made her wonder if he would mind that his most junior and newest employee had just taken on a case.

She paused before asking any more questions and tried to imagine what she would do if her sister Marie went missing. She would be worried but she would also be superfluous because her parents and Marie's husband would be heading the chase to find her. That was a point.

'Are your parents alive?' Jo asked. 'Do they have any ideas where he might be?'

'No, none at all.' Fitzpatrick was dismissive. 'And I don't know any of his friends all that well. I asked some discreet questions at the bank where he works but that didn't help. I'm glad you'll take this on anyway,' he added, 'I've realized there's a limit to what I can do on my own. I've been up here all morning and got nowhere—'

'What have you tried?' Jo asked out of interest.

'I asked at the bank to see if they could tell me what time he withdrew the money from the cash machine on the eighteenth but they wouldn't – a case of customer confidentiality, I think.'

Jo made a mental note to mention this to Macy. It was quite possible that he knew someone at the bank who would divulge this information.

'Then I went round the hospitals here,' Fitzpatrick was saying. 'I'd already tried the obvious London ones. But he's got to be somewhere, hasn't he? And I can't understand why he doesn't get in touch.'

'We'll do what we can,' Jo said bracingly. 'Do you have a photograph of him?'

She wondered what Sean was like. Could he be in

some sort of trouble? Had he left a boring job to run off with his girlfriend? Most importantly, when was he born?

Connor Fitzpatrick handed over a photograph of his brother. Jo looked at Sean's picture and saw a solid, square man standing, arms folded, on the drive of a large house. He was fair like Connor but broader and stockier and his face was a different shape: wider, more open and bland. His jawline was fleshy; his light eyes regarded the camera with a bored expression below springy brown hair. He was certainly not as attractive as his younger brother but appeared just as confident.

Fitzpatrick was looking at Jo curiously. 'You know, you seem a bit young to be running a place like this. Don't you mind?'

'Oh, I don't run it,' Jo laughed. She explained that it was just a part-time job while she tried to establish her own business as an astrologer. Fitzpatrick looked interested.

'Really? You can cast charts and say how people will be feeling next week? Is that it?'

This was as accurate a description of an astrologer's work as she had heard from a lay person and Jo was impressed. Most people tended to be superior about it, which was very irritating. 'It could be useful in finding out what's happened to your brother,' she suggested. 'I could work out Sean's natal chart for you, if you like, and from that it would be possible to know if he was going through a difficult time around the eighteenth.'

Fitzpatrick was enthusiastic and said he would get back to her with the details she would need about Sean's place and time of birth. 'But I can tell you straight away he's a Taurus. Does that help?'

'It surprises me,' Jo admitted. 'Taureans don't like change as a rule. They go for security and routine. If your brother just upped and went of his own accord, something must have made him willing to sacrifice all that.'

Fitzpatrick was shaking his head. 'It doesn't sound like Sean – what you say about him choosing the safe options. He likes security in the form of money well enough but he likes to take a few risks too, if you know what I mean. He has always been a bit of a daredevil – so I'm not convinced by astrology so far.' He smiled appealingly.

'You can't tell much from just his sun sign. That's the kind of thing that will come out in his chart,' Jo explained. 'I'll tell you more when I've worked it out.'

As Fitzpatrick happily agreed to pay for this additional work, she got the distinct impression that money was no problem. He stood up to go. 'Thanks for this,' he said warmly, 'I'm glad I happened to see this place. Just send me the bills, won't you? And will you ring me to keep in touch?'

'Yes, I'd want to come down to London,' Jo said. 'Ask some questions at his office, find out a bit more about Sean.'

'I'll give you their address,' Fitzpatrick said, producing a fountain pen and a leather-bound notebook, 'but I'd rather you didn't mention Sean's disappearance to anyone there. When he comes back to take up the reins he might prefer them to think he'd been ill. I'll give you the address of our house in Putney too. And the phone number in case you think of anything else to ask me about Sean.'

'Thanks.' Jo stood up to show Fitzpatrick out. 'One thing: what about your sun sign? What are you?'

'Can't you guess?' he grinned. But Jo was expecting this. The way he was constantly shifting his position and using his hands when he spoke, while his eyes wandered restlessly around the room, gave him away as a Gemini. He also had that strange mixture of diffidence and confidence, which she had noticed in other Geminis. She was often attracted to Geminis and Fitzpatrick was another example: she liked the easy way he talked and had the feeling that he couldn't be serious for long. In fact he probably couldn't be anything for long. She was about to make a confident guess when the door of the office opened and Macy walked in.

He stopped and looked around with an air of mild surprise. With his longish dark hair, jeans and loud summer shirt, he stood out in contrast to the neat, fair Fitzpatrick. Macy always had a slightly disreputable air, which made the difference between the two men even more marked. Jo suspected he was not pleased to find her installed behind his desk, particularly because she was talking to a client who was younger than him and better looking. As Macy was a Cancerian, it wouldn't matter to him that he had no justification or excuse to be jealous.

'I'm sorry, I didn't realize my office was engaged,' Macy said with a dark look at Jo. She was not deceived. The very pleasantness of his tone signified a sulk in the offing. Fitzpatrick looked blissfully unaware of the sins that had been committed and simply waited for Jo to introduce him, which she did. She explained briefly about the case. Macy nodded encouragingly, miming rapt attention. Jo thought he was overdoing it slightly. When she had finished he turned his attention to Fitzpatrick.

'Have you tried the Missing Persons' Bureau and the Salvation Army? And the local police here?' When Fitzpatrick shook his head, Macy went on. 'OK, that's where we can start then. Can I get you a coffee?'

'I was just about to go,' Fitzpatrick put in, 'Jo has been extremely helpful and she seems to have it all under control.'

'That's nice,' Macy said with his most charming smile. Jo showed Fitzpatrick out, leaving Macy to reclaim his office. There was only one way to deal with Macy in a bad mood, Jo had learned, and that was to go on the attack straight away.

'I got you some business there,' she said brightly when she went back into his office. Macy was ostentatiously moving things around on his desk as if they had been disturbed by a hurricane.

'Hmm. What about the reference checking?' he said irritably.

'I'll finish it at home. Is there anything you want to know about that man Fitzpatrick before I go?'

'No.' Macy gave her a brief look but as usual his eyes gave nothing away. Then he became deeply absorbed in some papers he had taken out of his briefcase. 'I'll put Alan on the case. And you can leave my notebook behind too.'

Jo dumped the notes on his desk. 'Oh well, suit yourself,' she said crisply, 'I have to go now. I'm going to London this evening.'

Once outside, she was annoyed that she had allowed herself to descend to Macy's childish level. Sometimes she said what she thought when she knew she would be better off keeping quiet: that was her Sagittarian ascendant. She should have remained superior and calmly voiced her objections to his giving Alan the case. She had won it, she felt, and she deserved it. She would have enjoyed finding out more about Sean Fitzpatrick's disappearance. And some more about his brother too, come to that: Connor Fitzpatrick aroused in Jo an interesting mixture of attraction and suspicion. She stopped her thoughts in their tracks. Seeing which way they were heading, she decided that it might not be a bad thing after all if she didn't get any further involved in this case. She didn't want to get mixed up with any unreliable Geminis.

Chapter Two

Jo had done all the research work she ever needed on attractive male Geminis. In fact she was meeting one that evening. She and Tim had lived together years ago when she had been working for a newspaper in Wales and Tim was a student. She had thought he was totally committed until she discovered he was giving the A-Level student he saw on Tuesday nights more than just special Maths tuition. Jo had forgotten the Gemini facility to do two things at once. Nowadays she and Tim were purely platonic and it was more relaxing. He was still a student but now living in London and she often stayed at his flat.

Connor Fitzpatrick's boyish charm had reminded her of Tim and she told herself she should steer clear. All the same she couldn't help feeling pleased when the case was unexpectedly handed back to her. She was battling to dry her bushy shoulder-length hair a couple of hours later when Alan rang. Since leaving the office she had been for her weekly swim with her friend Maurisha and it always had a bad effect on her hair.

'Jo, I want you to do me a favour.' Alan's voice was even more brusque than usual over the phone and he wasted no time on pleasantries. He worked for Macy full time. Jo disagreed with him about nearly everything. Despite this, they managed to tolerate each other very well.

'Did Macy tell you about this missing Irish bloke I'm

supposed to be looking for?' Alan wanted to know and Jo admitted she knew all about it. 'I've got a snowball's chance in hell of finding him,' he moaned. 'Does Macy realize that?'

'I know there wasn't much to go on. Just a woman called Rosie who might or might not live in Coventry and a date in June when he went to his bank – but you could check there first to see if that statement is correct. Otherwise this man may never have even come here—'

'I suppose it might be worth a try.' Alan was sceptical. 'Listen, Macy says you're going to London tonight. Are you? Because Macy wants me to go down too.'

Jo almost groaned aloud. Alan was only bearable in small doses. She was looking forward to her evening: she intended to go to a lecture held by the Astrological Society and stay at Tim's overnight. Alan didn't fit into these plans. But it turned out he had no desire to savour the delights of the capital. 'I hate the place,' he said vehemently. 'Don't know why so many people put up with working there. You used to, though, didn't you? You must know your way around? Are you staying over?'

'What do you want me to do?' Jo asked cautiously.

'It won't take long,' he promised. 'Macy wants me to go and see the missing bloke's parents. They won't speak to me on the phone. I was going to pop into the bank where he works as well but you might not have time for that. I'll give you a share of the pay of course.'

'OK – or you could do something for me in return,' Jo suggested. 'You know about cars, don't you?' She knew he did, even though he drove a rusted old Allegro. One of Alan's many jobs before joining the agency was as a car mechanic. Jo had bought her Renault 4 a week ago and it had started making an ominous knocking noise. She asked if Alan would have a look at it.

'Any time you like. Foreign rubbish of course,' he added cheerfully before ringing off. 'Told you to buy British, didn't I?'

Jo glared at the phone but she had to admit she felt a modicum of satisfaction that Alan had neatly dropped the Fitzpatrick case back into her lap. She guessed Macy would not be pleased. Going back to her make-up mirror, she gave herself a conspiratorial smile, which faded when she noticed her hair.

She had failed to tame it into good behaviour. It was wavy and dark and difficult, in her opinion. She had inherited it from her father, who described himself as a Welsh Italian, although he had moved to Coventry before Jo was born. Jo's eyes were grey like her father's and she liked to think she looked a bit Celtic. But she could have done without the abundant hair.

She had to rush to the station. She couldn't trust her car on long journeys since it had started to knock. Once on the train with a cup of British Rail coffee slopping around in front of her, she dug out the ephemeris for 1960, which she had stuffed in her duffle bag. This told her the position of the planets on the day Sean Fitzpatrick was born. It gave her a starting point but no more. She would need to know exactly when he was born and where before she could work out his natal chart. Sean had three important planets in Aries, which would certainly make him more selfish, decisive and quick-tempered than the average Taurean. And Venus was in Pisces, which meant he was excitable and easily bored. Not a typical contented Taurus at all. Jo itched to be able to get on with the rest of his chart.

As she couldn't, she went over the story Connor Fitzpatrick had told her. She thought of it as a story because she didn't entirely believe it. But it must at least be true that his brother had disappeared, and that was what interested her. Why would someone just up and go like that? Was he running from or to something? And what had prompted him to leave on that particular morning?

Chapter Three

As a member of the Astrological Society, Jo was entitled to attend the monthly lectures at the college in Russell Square and she usually managed to go. Tonight an expert on horary astrology was speaking and Jo didn't entirely agree with him.

'You can cast a chart to answer any question,' the lecturer said, throwing his arms expansively. 'By assuming the question comes into being the moment it is asked, it is possible to deduce the answer from the planets—'

Jo was dubious. Like most astrologers she didn't believe astrology could predict the future in specific terms. If only it was as easy as that, she could tell from the position of the planets what exactly was on Sean's mind the moment he left the house on that Friday morning. She decided she should stick to analysing his natal chart because she knew she could do that well.

After the lecture she spent the rest of the evening with Tim and he wanted to tell her all about his differences of opinion with his tutor. So it wasn't until the following day when she was on the Tube heading east across London that she was able to give Sean Fitzpatrick the concentration he deserved. She balanced a new notebook on her knee and tried to reconstruct the notes she had left at Macy's.

Sean Fitzpatrick's office was in the City in one of those narrow roads where office blocks of different decades are squashed uneasily together. It took some finding, which Jo had not anticipated. She had thought the offices of a big clearing bank like the National Commercial would be more imposing than the anonymous ten-storey building she eventually found.

It took a minute for her eyes to adjust from the bright sunlight outside to the dim interior. She successfully negotiated her way past the dark glass coffee tables and black leather seats to the desk at the back, where a woman watched her progress expectantly from behind a spotlit desk. Probably this woman's sole entertainment was watching temporarily blinded people crash into plate-glass tables, Jo thought.

'Have you an appointment?' Jo was asked in cool tones.

'I've come to see Sean Fitzpatrick.'

'What section?'

'I'm sorry, I don't know.'

The woman consulted a list and then looked up at Jo with an understanding smile. 'Oh yes. I'll let them know you're here.'

Jo started to say that no one was expecting her but the woman had turned away to make a call. Jo gave up. Often it was better just to let events take their course. She sat on one of the leather chairs and sank so deep she couldn't see how she was going to get up without displaying her upper thighs to the world. After a minute or two, the woman came over with some papers. She looked surprisingly normal without her desk.

'Would you like to fill this in while you wait? Mr Walmsley will send someone down for you in about twenty minutes.'

'What about Mr Fitzpatrick?' Jo asked disingenuously. 'I specifically came to see him.'

'I'm afraid he's not in today. Don't worry, Mr Walmsley is from the same section.'

Jo thanked her and wondered what she was getting

into. Were they expecting a new managing director to start today? Well, perhaps it's time I had a career change, she thought. Then she saw she was holding an application form – but for which job? Still, she had twenty minutes to kill so she dutifully filled in the form – and quite honestly too – though she did not say she was a private investigator, giving her old civil service job as her current employment. She was just ploughing through the section on how she saw herself in five years' time when a well-groomed young man appeared from the lift opposite and came over to her. He introduced himself as Vaz Harri. Jo handed him the form and he looked through it.

'I didn't have time to finish it, I'm afraid,' Jo heard herself say apologetically and had to smile to herself. Old habits die hard, she thought. She had applied for all sorts of jobs in the past and had to remind herself that this was not for real.

Vaz was smiling back at her. 'That's fine,' he said. 'Follow me, I'll show you around. We are seeing about thirty people today and hope to get a shortlist for a formal interview next week. I see you have not worked in banking before?'

Jo had to admit this was true but she had done various office jobs and said so as she followed Vaz into the lift. He asked her about them in a friendly, laconic manner as they travelled up to the ninth floor and through an open-plan office. She walked along the noisy corridor past staring computer screens and desks covered with papers and was reminded strongly of the strange enclosed world of office life.

'Do you know Sean Fitzpatrick?' she asked Vaz when he returned to her side.

'Yes, he works here,' Vaz nodded towards an office door, 'but he's not in today. Why? Do you know him?'

'Yes, he told me about the job,' Jo said glibly.

'Oh, did he?' Vaz gave a disconcerting look. 'You should have as good a chance as anybody, then.'

Jo wondered what that was supposed to mean. 'Is he off sick, then?' she persevered.

'I think so,' Vaz said carefully. He pulled out a chair for her near one of the desks. 'I'll tell you a bit about the job now,' he said, sitting down and looking at some papers in front of him.

Jo listened as he launched into an explanation of the vacancy, which he had probably had to repeat thirty times that day. It was clerical work, involving keeping computer records up to date. Jo looked around covertly. This was a quiet corner of the floor, with only Vaz and a woman at the desk opposite and no phones ringing. Not far away were office doors, one of which might belong to Sean. Jo would have dearly liked to take a look in there.

'Do you enjoy working here?' she asked Vaz when he seemed to have come to an end.

Vaz hesitated. 'Of course,' he answered. He looked suddenly less assured and she realized he was probably a few years younger than her.

'A lot of people don't like their jobs,' she said conversationally. 'Is this a good place to work? Things going on socially?'

'Oh yes.' Vaz gave a relieved smile. 'On this section, we go out for meals and we're all pretty friendly at work—' He had already explained that he and Donna, the woman opposite, worked for Mr Fitzpatrick and above him, Mr Walmsley.

'And you all get on well?' Jo asked casually. 'Even with the bosses?'

'Very well,' Vaz replied. 'Nick Walmsley is great to work for—'

'What about Sean?' Jo asked and tried to soften the question by adding, 'Some bosses are so difficult, aren't they?'

'He's very friendly too,' Vaz answered.

Jo felt there was a certain constraint in this reply but there were no chances to find out any more until Vaz showed her out. When they were in the lift, Jo asked him how well he knew Sean Fitzpatrick. She felt she had nothing to lose now. Vaz looked at her curiously.

'I wish I knew why you are so interested in him,' Vaz commented, watching the display panel over the lift door as it showed the descending floor numbers.

'What do you mean?' Jo asked, wondering how much she should tell him.

'Well, let's put it like this,' Vaz said as the lift came to a halt. 'If your interest is professional, then you should ask someone more on his level – I'm just an underling,' he added with a small smile. 'If it is personal...' He stepped out of the lift.

'Go on,' Jo said, following him through the dim foyer.

When they had walked a few paces past the reception desk, Vaz looked at her. 'Well, if you were a friend of mine and you were thinking of being interested in him personally,' he said slowly, 'I would say don't, that's all.' He stopped at the front doors and shrugged his shoulders. 'You probably won't take my advice anyway.'

'I'm not sure I understand it,' Jo said, wanting him to explain further.

Vaz smiled and pushed the glass doors open for her. 'You do,' he said confidently. 'I hope to see you again soon.'

Jo stepped out into the street, blinking again. Well, that was something and nothing, she thought to herself. Now for lunch.

'A man's body,' she heard Macy say. 'What, a *dead* body?' he repeated, somewhat needlessly, she thought. She looked up but he was listening and nodding, which didn't tell her anything.

'Do you want to see a body?' he asked as soon as he put the phone down.

'It wouldn't be my first choice of entertainment,' Jo was saying as Macy, moving quickly for him, picked up his car keys on the way out.

'The police have found a body in Gollins Wood, do you know it?' he said as he left the office and went down the stairs. Celia stared after them, indignant that anyone should pass her desk without speaking.

'Yes, it's near Princethorpe – not far,' Jo answered. She had to follow him down the dingy corridor at the back of the building to find out more.

'They called me because they knew we were looking for Fitzpatrick and apparently this could be him,' Macy said as he led the way through the back door of the office to the narrow alley where his car was parked. 'They think we might be able to help identify it.'

'Alan will be mad at missing this,' Jo commented lightly as Macy manoeuvred the old Cortina out of an impossibly small space.

'Damn. I should have told Celia where he could find us.' Macy stopped the car halfway through the ten-point turn and ran back to the office. When he came back he was carrying Fitzpatrick's file. He dropped it on Jo's lap. 'This might come in handy too. See if you can dig out his photograph.'

'Did they say what had happened to this body?' Jo asked as she looked through the thin folder.

'They said some kids found it half-buried in the woods.'

'I don't see why it should be Sean.' Jo looked at his photograph: a boy next door type with mousy hair and nondescript eyes. Not a handsome face, nor a complicated one, she thought. Jo mentally prepared herself as

Chapter Four

Jo bought some peanut butter and banana sandwiches and ate them on the train to Richmond. Sitting in a half-empty carriage with the window down to let a cool breeze in, she thought about Vaz. She had instinctively liked him. She had decided he was probably a Virgo like herself and she took to him because he seemed efficient, reserved and not one to suffer fools gladly.

Pity she couldn't have got more out of him about Sean, she thought, but it was difficult to ask searching questions when she had promised Connor not to mention that his brother had disappeared. Vaz had hinted that Sean Fitzpatrick was bad news for women. Something Connor Fitzpatrick had said had given Jo a similar impression. But this was not enlightening. After all, what man wasn't, she thought cynically. Maybe Sean's parents would help to flesh out his character.

The Fitzpatricks lived just off Richmond Hill, on a quiet road where most of the houses looked deceptively ordinary. Jo guessed they actually belonged to film directors and orthodontists. She had found the place easily enough. Alan had given her the address. Her battered and somewhat out of date *A-Z* had done the rest and she was walking up the drive by four o'clock, which she reckoned was pretty good going. The house was a square, symmetrical Georgian building of pale brick and long windows and something about the place gave her a sense of *déjà-vu*. As she rang the tastefully quiet doorbell, the reason came to her: in his photograph, Sean Fitzpatrick had been standing on the pink gravel drive.

A middle-aged woman came to the door and opened it just wide enough for her to see out with dignity. She wore a suit in expensive dingy colours and looked at Jo with a vague distrust, not quite hidden by a thin smile.

'Mrs Fitzpatrick?' Jo asked tentatively because she felt that anyone who could afford to live in a house like this would be unlikely to open the door themselves. But she was wrong. The older woman nodded and continued to look at Jo cautiously.

'I was speaking to your son yesterday—'

'Which one?' Mrs Fitzpatrick asked crisply.

'Connor. He said you might be able to help. He's very concerned about Sean. Do you mind if I come in?' Jo hoped to get inside the house. Interviews on doorsteps were hopeless. People were always distracted and preoccupied and their means of escape was too accessible.

'I won't be able to tell you anything about Sean's whereabouts,' Mrs Fitzpatrick said discouragingly. 'Are you another of the private investigators Connor has hired? I had one rude individual ring me up last night.'

'It won't take long, honestly,' Jo said with false cheerfulness, hoping to gloss over Alan's misdemeanours. 'If I could just come in—'

Mrs Fitzpatrick grudgingly agreed, specifying that she only had ten minutes to spare. Jo, silently victorious, followed the tall woman down her spacious hall. She had a slim build and a conscious grace: even her high heels tapped a well-modulated rhythm on the shiny parquet. Her clothes and make-up were immaculate. Joe had a close scrutiny of both as Mrs Fitzpatrick opened a door to let Jo go ahead of her. It was the bone structure that made her look so striking. Mrs Fitzpatrick had the same high cheek bones and deep, narrow eyes as Connor. With that willowy figure, Jo guessed that she had been gorgeous not so long ago.

'Will you sit down?' Mrs Fitzpatrick asked with formal politeness. 'I'm Fiona Fitzpatrick, by the way. You are?'

Jo introduced herself before she sat down on a chair which was covered in a bold striped fabric. The room, at the back of the house, smelled faintly of dried flowers and polish. It seemed to be used as an office except the desk was a large fancy bureau and the computer was on a cherrywood dining-table. Hardly standard office furniture, Jo thought. The windows were heavily draped, which made it dark. Mrs Fitzpatrick did not sit but leant against the table, where her discreet bottom gently dislodged some papers from the pile there.

'When did you last see Sean?' Jo asked, watching as a single page floated to the carpet. Fiona Fitzpatrick did not bother to pick it up.

'About a month ago. He came for Sunday lunch, which he does once a month.' She sighed. 'I hope Connor knows what he's doing. I don't really see how you can help.'

'It is mainly what we do: tracing people. We are good at it.' This woman's superior air made Jo feel defensive. 'The police won't do much about a missing person if there are no suspicious circumstances. Connor seems to be very worried about his brother—'

'Yes, he does, doesn't her?' Fiona Fitzpatrick gave Jo a look of amused tolerance like someone who is watching a sport she doesn't understand. 'Why do you think that is?' she asked, continuing to look at Jo. 'Or don't you ask yourselves questions like that if someone is paying the bill?'

Jo ignored the question and instead asked, 'Are *you* worried about your son, Mrs Fitzpatrick?'

'I gave up wondering if he had a hot dinner and a clean shirt long before he left home and that was ten years ago.' Jo noticed the slight Irish accent for the first time. Mrs Fitzpatrick ostentatiously looked at her watch and Jo felt she must plough on with her questions. She knew so little about Sean, virtually any question would do.

'Did he leave home to share a house with Connor?'

'No, Connor was at Oxford then. Sean left to get married and settle down.' Mrs Fitzpatrick finished on a laugh.

Jo failed to see the joke. 'He's not married any more?'

'No,' came the short answer.

'Can you let me have the name and address of his ex-wife?'

'She was called Valerie. I have no idea where she is now.'

Jo made a mental note to ask Connor. 'Where do you think Sean might be?' she tried.

Fiona Fitzpatrick pulled at a long silver pendant around her neck and looked past Jo. She shrugged elegantly. 'Sidney? Rio? The Orkneys? Your guess is as good as mine. Now I must remind you, I said a few minutes only. I have to ask you to go.' She gave the impression of someone who had done their painful duty. Smug and indifferent would be the two words to choose between, Jo thought, if she was asked to sum up Mrs F. in one.

'I suppose you remember him being born?' Jo stood up, glancing round the room and taking in the expensive clutter.

'Sorry?' Fiona Fitzpatrick sounded gratifyingly puzzled by the change of tack.

Jo went over to a waist-high urn of dried flowers in the hearth as if drawn to the arrangement. In fact she had noticed some family photographs on the mantelpiece and wanted to get a discreet look. 'Lovely display,' Jo murmured.

'What do you mean about remembering Sean's birth?' the other woman said irritably.

'I know he's not the eldest, but do you remember him being born?' The photographs were all dull studio portraits of various family members. Jo picked out the ones she knew. Connor was there, his pointed chin and sexy blue eyes looking ingenuously over his mother's shoulder. She recognized Sean, standing straight, uncompromising and none too happy between what must be his father and elder brother. They were both well built and swarthy and noticeably father and son.

'I think it's time for you to go—' Fiona Fitzpatrick's heels were tapping towards the door.

'Oh. Yes,' Jo agreed absently, 'I just wondered if you could tell me when Sean was born. The exact time and place, if possible.' Jo turned to face the other woman and smiled politely, adding that she was an astrologer and had promised to cast Sean's horoscope.

'I despair of Connor, I really do,' Fiona sighed, frowning at her. Making it obvious she thought the whole idea was nonsense, she nevertheless gave the necessary information. Jo noted it down, tempted to ask for Connor's details too, but she decided not to push her luck.

'What about your husband, could he help me?' Jo said, taking her time on her journey back to the front door.

'I don't think you would want to wait for him. He will not be home until eleven tonight,' Mrs Fitzpatrick said, adding quietly, 'if then.'

'Perhaps I could see him at work?' Jo felt it was worth a try. She stopped in front of a sombre watercolour in the hall.

'Oh yes, he would love a chat about his favourite son over the operating table.'

The older woman's sarcasm was a little heavy, Jo thought. 'Your husband's a doctor?' She smiled blandly.

'A consultant.' Mrs Fitzpatrick stepped past Jo and pointedly opened the front door. 'But I really don't advise you to contact him. He has even less interest in this business than I do.'

It was the nearest Jo had ever come to being thrown out and as she walked back to the station, she found herself getting angrier about it. Fiona Fitzpatrick had so obviously looked down her nose. Even if the woman couldn't give a damn if her son was alive or dead, there was no need to be so rude. Her superciliousness grated far more than a string of insults would have done and gradually, waiting for the train, Jo began to feel annoyed with Connor Fitzpatrick as well. After all, if he was going to employ private investigators to find his brother, you would think he could at least persuade his mother to be civil to them, she thought.

By the time her train had stopped at Putney, Jo had found Connor's address in her handbag but when she rang the bell of his terraced house there was no answer. She stood in the brick storm porch and looked up and down the street. There were plenty of people about but no sign of Connor. She looked at her watch and realized he would probably still be at work. She had three choices, as she saw it: to give up and get the train back to Coventry; to go to Connor's office and hope to catch him there; or to wait for him to come home. Of course he could be hours. She tried the doorbell again. The black venetian blinds on the bay window meant that she could not see in.

After waiting a few more minutes, she started back down the street. At the end was a public telephone. She dug in her handbag again for change and rang directory enquiries. She had left Connor's business card in Macy's office but she remembered the name of the firm and had no trouble getting the number. She rang it and asked to speak to Connor. A man told her he had left for the day.

It was half-past five. If Connor came straight home, he would be here soon. Jo wandered down Putney High Street and went in to a pizzeria to get the cup of coffee she had been craving since lunch time. She decided it was worth waiting as long as it took to drink a coffee. She had no reason to be home early.

Her spirits were improved by the dose of caffeine and she felt another lift as she walked back up Chiltern Street and saw a new Peugeot outside Connor's house which had not been there before. She rang the doorbell confidently. Beside her she saw the blinds shudder. Then Connor, looking more rumpled than when she had last seen him, with his tie loose and his shoes in his hands, came to the door.

'Jo!' he said, remembering her and sounding pleased about it. 'Are you on the case? Have you come to interrogate me? Come in and have a drink—'

He was more hospitable than his mother, anyway. Jo smiled at Connor and, seeing how easy it was to succumb to his obvious charm, had to remind herself that she was annoyed with him.

'I was just fixing myself a teeny little gin. How about you?' Connor led the way into the front room.

Jo accepted the offer of a drink and took a seat on an impractically white sofa while he went to get it. The room was austere and monochrome. The minimalist style, apart from being dated, did not go with the house, Jo decided. She picked up some envelopes which lay on the sofa beside her: just bills and circulars. They didn't tell her any more about Connor or Sean than the room did.

'So have you come to give me a progress report, or what?' Connor asked as he handed her a heavy glass, which clinked with ice. 'Do you know where he is yet?' He sat down on a very uncomfortable-looking armchair across the room.

Jo shook her head. 'I'm afraid not,' she had to admit. 'But we've only just started. I'm still trying to put together a picture of him in my head.' While she was still a bit annoyed with Connor, Jo told him about the visit to his mother's. 'I think you should have told her to co-operate with the investigation,' she finished, feeling better already for having unloaded her irritation.

Connor lifted his hands. 'What can I do? I'm sorry, but did she look to you like the kind of woman you could tell how to behave?' He reached for the gin bottle and topped up Jo's drink and his own. 'She can be difficult, I know.'

Jo felt sympathetic because she might have had a similar problem with her own mother but she tried not to let this show. 'But she doesn't seem terribly worried about Sean?'

'She subscribes to the school of thought which says if a grown man wants to opt out of his life temporarily then let him,' Connor sighed.

'And you don't?'

'No,' he answered surprisingly sharply. 'Not when he owes me money, I don't.'

Jo took a sip of her drink so that she didn't appear to pounce on this information. 'Much?' she asked casually.

Connor stood up and wandered towards the window. 'No, not really.'

'Is that why you want us to find him?'

'He does pay half the mortgage, which isn't exactly peanuts. Apart from that – well – yes – money is part of the reason. I don't want to go into it all now.' He lifted a slat of the blind to look out. 'Tell you what – why don't we eat?' He turned round to smile at Jo. 'Italian? Thai? Indian? What would you prefer?'

It was seriously tempting but Jo had reservations about getting too involved with Connor. She reminded herself that he was a Gemini and so could probably talk her into anything after a few glasses of wine. Virtuously, she said she would have to go back to Coventry and should make a start soon. 'There are a couple more things you could help me with, though. Sean had been married, hadn't he? Do you know how we can contact his ex-wife?'

'No point.' Connor tipped back his head to finish his drink. 'Valerie left him years ago. I think she's in New Zealand now. She got a job with a travel firm and ended up there.'

'Why did he get divorced?'

'Oh, I don't know. These things happen.' Connor shrugged easily. Jo waited, sipping at the iced water, which was all that was left of her drink. Geminis can't bear long silences.

Connor fiddled with the blinds and paced back to the centre of the room. 'What do you want to know this old history for? Sean's divorce was eight years ago or more.' He looked at Jo and laughed suddenly. 'Well, I can see you're not going to give up. Sean and Valerie were not married all that long – about two years. He gave her a very bad time, apparently. That was one of the reasons the family fell out with him. I was up at Oxford at the time so I never really found out about it.'

'And she's working abroad now?' Jo weighed this up for a moment and then asked: 'Could I have a look at Sean's room?'

'Sure.' Connor led the way upstairs, still carrying his empty glass. 'I've looked through the papers and stuff he left behind. I couldn't find anything to tell me where he was going – except that one bank statement that mentioned Coventry.'

Sean's bedroom was at the front of the house and he had a desk in the bay window. The room was not as tidy as the one downstairs but it was more comfortable, as Jo expected, knowing Sean was a Taurean. A squashy old armchair took up one corner with stereo speakers placed either side of it. There was a jumper on the bed, papers on the desk and coins, books and pens on the bedside table. The books in the room were all financial reference books or text books. Jo slid back the doors of the wardrobe, while Connor watched silently. Hanging up were suits, jackets, shirts, belts, ties. There were two suitcases and an empty hold-all stacked neatly at the back. The white chest of drawers was also full of clothes. It was not the room of someone who had made a planned departure.

'All his belongings are here, then?' Jo asked, looking

around. There was one picture on the wall: a rather soulless black and white photograph of clouds.

'As far as I can tell.'

Jo moved over to the desk. 'Do you mind if I look—?'

'Go ahead.' Connor followed her to the window and stood looking out at the street. There were blinds in this room too but he could see out without adjusting them. Jo leaned over the desk, where it looked like Sean had been working on his accounts. There were long print-outs showing lists of debits and credits, bank statements, credit card statements for various cards and hand-written sums on scraps of paper.

Jo picked up one of the credit card bills. It seemed Sean spent a lot of money on clothes and petrol. She recognized the address of one garage on the A46 near Coventry, where he had bought petrol on May 17. So his visit of June 18 might not have been a one-off. She took her notebook out of her handbag and scribbled down the address, although she didn't think it would get her anywhere.

She cast an eye down the print-outs. The details of each transaction were very sketchy and she couldn't deduce much from them. Certainly Sean spent a lot of money but he also had a lot coming in. She picked up a plastic credit card holder which was lying on the desk and flicked through it. There were one or two account cards for major retailers and some membership cards. One was for a gym in the City, two were for casinos in Knightsbridge and one, which Jo flicked past and then turned back for a closer look, was for a sports club in Leamington Spa. The club was called Greenaways. She had never heard of the place but Leamington was less than half an hour from Coventry. And it was off the A46.

'Have you looked through all this stuff?' Jo asked as she picked up some more bills.

'Not really.' Connor was still staring expressionlessly out of the window. 'I had a quick look but all I found were endless bills he's run up in clubs and restaurants, which I knew anyway. You find anything else?'

'No, that's about all there is,' she agreed, slipping the Greenaways card into her handbag. She didn't know why she didn't want Connor to know everything just yet but she trusted her instinct. She noted down the names of the casinos to pass on to Alan or Macy.

'Have you finished in here now?' Connor asked testily.

'Yes, thanks.'

'Believe me, I've had a good look round. These are mainly just papers from the bank. He used to bring a lot of work home.'

'Was he doing very well in his career?' Jo asked as they went downstairs.

'Not as well as he should have been—' Somewhere in the house a phone started ringing and Connor stopped speaking. He hesitated with one hand on the bannister. 'Don't answer it,' he said quietly and then looking up at Jo and laughing over the ringing sound, he added, 'I mean, I've left the answering machine on. So there's no need.'

The answering machine must have cut in because the phone had stopped ringing by the time they reached the hall. Connor looked less relaxed than Jo had ever seen him before. She refused his offer of another drink but she thought he looked like he needed one and said so.

'I'm just not used to living on my own.' He grinned self-consciously. 'I do get a little jumpy.'

It was true that he did seem to be a bit on edge but perhaps that was understandable since his brother had gone missing, Jo thought as she walked to the Tube station. Anyway it explained why Connor was showing all this brotherly concern if Sean owed him money. Maybe they were both in debt and that was why Sean had made himself scarce? She wondered why Sean had gone to Coventry on June 18 and whether he was still there. Perhaps with his girlfriend Rosie? But she had not seen anything personal among Sean's papers: no letters or cards and no clue to Rosie's identity or whereabouts. It was a wild guess that she was the link between Sean and Coventry.

The only definite link was in Jo's handbag. She took out the plastic membership card for the club in Leamington: *Greenaways: a Lifestyle Club. Fine facilities in gracious surroundings.* Jo congratulated herself privately. So what if she had nearly been thrown out by a snobby woman and had spent half the day hanging around waiting for trains? She had her first real lead.

Chapter Five

Jo had arranged to meet Alan at Macy's early the next morning so that she could tell him what she had found out. She regretted this when her alarm clock went off and wished she had not stayed up until 3 a.m. working on Sean's chart. She showered, made coffee and munched a bowl of cereal, which she considered to be very boring food. She ate it for the same reason she went swimming: because it was good for her. She fed Preston the cat and left her flat at eight thirty, hurrying down the fire escape to the back of the house, where her car was parked.

At eight forty-five she abandoned all hope of driving to work. All she could get out of the car when she turned the ignition key was a disheartening click. There was not even the satisfaction of revving the engine. Just a click. Jo, naturally, got out and looked under the bonnet but she had only a slim idea what she was looking at. She fiddled with a couple of wires attached to the battery and tried again. Nothing – except the click. Gloomily she locked up the car and began the short walk into the centre of Coventry.

Her mind was going over various car problems trying to guess how much they would cost to sort out, so it was not until she was walking down the Burges, the busy, narrow street where the agency was discreetly situated over a shoe shop, that she remembered she and Macy had fallen out. She wondered if he was still sulking as she pushed open the blue door and climbed the steep stairs to the first floor. She really preferred to be on good terms with Macy although they could never seem to maintain it for long.

'Jo! How are you? Did you have a good time in London?' Celia seemed pleased to see her as usual.

'I'm fine but the car's sick. Anybody in?' Jo asked, taking a seat in one of the old armchairs by Celia's desk.

'Yes, Mr Macy's in his office. I expect he'll be out in a minute to say hello.'

'I doubt it.' Jo accepted a coffee from Celia. 'He's not happy with me at the moment. Do you know if anything has happened on this missing person case? Sean Fitzpatrick.'

'What have you done to upset Mr Macy?' Celia grinned at Jo conspiratorially, as she reached for the filing cabinet drawer, bracelets jangling. She flicked through various files and pulled one out.

'The other day when I was working in his room, he came in and found me. On top of that I had dealt with a client, which led to us getting this Fitzpatrick case,' Jo explained.

'Unforgivable.' Celia shook her head in mock disapproval. 'Now, Fitzpatrick...' She looked down at the file notes. 'Mr Macy informed the police on Wednesday afternoon but they weren't able to help. Alan has yet to report—'

She was interrupted by Macy appearing from his office. He had a long thin body; his hair and eyes were the same muddy brown. Even when he wore a suit and tie like today, his clothes tended to look crumpled and untucked. Despite this, he still managed to be attractive. Jo tried to ignore it but she knew he felt the same about her. They had made love once on a rainy evening in front of the gas fire in her flat. But instead of feeling closer to him, Jo found it easier to revert to their friendly – if uneasy – business relationship afterwards.

Macy was leaning against the door frame and looked

at her expectantly. 'Got us any more business lately? Anyone bumped into you in the street and begged you to find their long-lost cousin? Or—'

'Sarcasm: the refuge of the desperate man,' Jo asserted, smiling triumphantly.

Macy shot her a quick humorous look. 'The question is: is it worth my paying your expenses to London? Alan told me he'd asked you to go.' He pushed open the door of his office and Jo followed him in, aware that Celia was grinning with satisfaction.

Jo described her meeting with Mrs Fitzpatrick and her visit to the National Commercial Bank. 'But you don't have to pay me,' she finished, 'Alan and I did a deal.'

Macy didn't argue or ask for explanations. He wrote down the names of casinos Sean visited and said he would check them out.

'I found those in Sean's bedroom,' Jo went on, 'I had a quick look when I called to see Connor. He said that Sean owed him money but he didn't tell me how much.'

'So what have you found out about Sean Fitzpatrick? In ten words.'

'He's tough, clever – very ambitious. People like him but he uses them and he's probably promiscuous too.'

'Did you get that from an ex-girlfriend?' Macy asked with characteristic cynicism.

'No. From his chart,' Jo responded smartly. 'He's Taurus with Sagittarius rising and the Moon in Aries.'

She predicted that Macy was going to make some flippant comment but he was interrupted by the phone ringing. Celia put a call through.

'Police,' Macy said to Jo briefly before the line was connected. She was not particularly curious. PI work necessarily overlaps with police work from time to time and she knew Macy had some good contacts in the Coventry station. She only half listened. Privately, she was pleased that she and Macy were back on their usual terms.

they drove out of the city. She had seen a dead body only once before. She had managed to forget the details but remembered the experience and was glad she had only eaten cereal that morning.

Macy drove to Princethorpe, which was a sizeable village east of the city, and then demanded directions. Jo directed him through the village and down an unsignposted narrow lane. Macy didn't argue. Jo was a local and he wasn't. She had lived in Coventry all her life until she had left to go to university and it had not changed much in the seven years since then. She knew Princethorpe as a place with a good pub but the wood was quite a long way from the village, near the reservoir, if she remembered correctly. The surrounding area was largely agricultural but some of the woods and hedgerows were still intact and their branches battered the car on both sides as Macy tore along the lanes. On Jo's instructions he turned right on to a B-road, which was wider and busier, and then right again.

'This is it,' Macy murmured when the first police car came in sight, parked with two wheels on the grass verge. He pulled the Cortina in behind it and he and Jo walked in silence up the lane.

Jo could see the garish yellow of rape flowers through the hedge on one side of them. Their sickly oily smell seemed to stick in her chest. On their right was Gollins Wood. Jo had remembered it as a small, pretty, typically English wood. Today it seemed dense and tall. Ahead of them was commotion. They passed several police cars and heard the hiss of voices on a radio before they could distinguish the words.

'Hold on.' A police constable got out of a car in front and held up his hand. 'You can't go up there just now.'

'Detective Sergeant Beatty asked me to come,' Macy said. The constable thought about it for a moment and then waved them on as if he was on point duty. Further down the road there were more vehicles, including a van, which was parked with two more police cars in a lay-by. Jo scanned them for a red Ford Escort GTI, which was Sean Fitzpatrick's car, but it wasn't there. This lay-by and the path leading off into the woods seemed to be the hub of all the activity. The people who milled around purposefully must all be police, Jo assumed, whether in or out of uniform. Macy was making a beeline for a woman with a short skirt and a clipboard. This turned out to be Detective Sergeant Beatty.

'The body's about fifty metres into the woods. Don't go in,' she added although neither Macy nor Jo had made a move towards the woods. 'They'll be bringing it out in a minute,' she went on rapidly. 'Shallow grave and it's been chewed about a bit I'm afraid.'

Jo's stomach lurched alarmingly. She fixed her feet firmly on the trampled grass and locked her eyes on the footpath leading into the woods. A man in a suit tramped along it towards them. The bottoms of his trousers were covered in mud. 'Dr Chapple says blow to the back of the head,' he muttered to Sergeant Beatty. 'Dead some days. Food for the foxes, which are a bloody pest around here. Did you get hold of that PI with the picture?'

Sergeant Beatty looked round for them. 'Have you got a photo, David?' she said to Macy. David? Jo tried not to look surprised. Macy's contacts with the local police must be even better than she had thought.

'Sorry. I couldn't bring a photo. One of my investigators has it,' Macy was saying. 'He may be along later.'

The man in the suit raised his eyes to the glorious blue sky. Jo said nothing but folded her arms over the Fitzpatrick file. She guessed Macy did not admit to having the photograph because he thought they would then be summarily dismissed. Through the narrow gap between the trees, Jo could see an ordered procession approaching. Two constables led the way carrying large black sacks. Behind them were men carrying a stretcher. It seemed to be heavy and their feet slithered on the mud.

The first thing Jo noticed was that the body was not covered up. She could see the dead man's trousers, ripped at the ankle – or maybe bitten? His leg was visible: a white, hairy, muscular calf mangled and smeared with blood and mud. Jo's arms were tensed like steel around the file. She felt they were holding her up. The wavering, uncertain progress of the horizontal body drew nearer.

When the stretcher was within touching distance, Sergeant Beatty put a hand out and spoke to the man holding the front of the stretcher. Jo didn't hear what was said, she was staring down at the dirty white face which seemed to hover below her. The lips were pulled back in a frozen grimace and Jo could see the white teeth. The top of the head was a horrible flattened shape covered by matted hair and dried blood.

Jo was having trouble associating this muddy, torn body with the man she had been looking for all day yesterday. And yet at the same time she was sure it was Sean Fitzpatrick. It was something about the square shape of the jaw.

'I'm pretty sure it's him,' she heard Macy say. If Macy hadn't spoken, Jo would have. She watched the stretcher being lifted into the mortuary van.

It was not that she hadn't considered that Sean might be dead. In fact that was one of the first things that had occurred to her when she had heard Connor Fitzpatrick's story. Car crash or suicide, she had thought clinically. But her job had been to delve into Sean's life. Now, having seen his dead body she found herself thinking of the mundane glimpses she had seen of it: his elegant mother, his comfortably untidy bedroom, his office, where his colleagues were mildly curious about his absence, slightly critical about his reputation with women. They were going on thinking of him as being alive.

She had spent hours analysing his character last night and had put out of her mind the thought that she might be casting a dead person's chart. Sean's chart had not endeared him to her. He came over as something of a bully. Mercury in Aries in the fifth house, together with a Sagittarius ascendant, confirmed he had been a gambler and there were indications that this could easily have become a compulsion. On the plus side, he had been bright, decisive and enterprising – and a good communicator. But a badly afflicted Venus meant his attitude to women had left something to be desired: he had tended to see them as possessions. Jo had not got as far as progressing the chart to see what the future had in store for Sean. It was a good job she hadn't bothered, she thought blackly.

She stood very still while her brain stumbled through these confused thoughts. Beside her Macy was equally immobile. They were unwilling to look up and acknowledge the other's presence. It was as if they both felt they could only deal with this by pretending they were alone.

Eventually Sergeant Beatty came up to Macy and thanked him, which was obviously meant to be their dismissal. Macy chatted with her for a minute, asking her questions which she mainly avoided answering, until she was called away. Very gradually, Jo lessened the tension in her arms and legs. A hand fell on her shoulder and a cheerful voice said loudly in her ear, 'It's all happening, isn't it? Have I missed the big event?'

'What the hell are you doing?' Jo snapped, swinging round, to confront Alan's impervious grin. She had known it was him. Only one person could generate such enthusiasm when faced with a possible murder. But she was still angry. 'Don't sneak up on me like that. No, it wasn't that much fun,' she told him.

'And yes you are late,' Macy added. 'You have missed the body. It looked like Fitzpatrick to me.'

'You mean they let you get close up?' Alan asked, impressed. 'I thought they would just take the photo off you and do the identity bit themselves.'

'I said I didn't have the photo,' Macy sighed.

'Quite right,' Alan said approvingly. 'Gone off to the morgue, has it?' He looked round curiously, as if he half hoped to see the body lying around. At least Alan, with his usual lack of sensitivity, had jolted them out of inactivity, Jo realized.

Macy started back to the car. 'I suppose we may as well try to do something useful for our client. Why don't you two stay around here for a while?' he said. 'The police are going to fetch Connor from London. They need a formal identification. I'd better offer to go and see the body with him.'

'The police won't tell us anything,' Jo said discouragingly.

'Well, Fitzpatrick must have come from somewhere. There didn't seem to be a car,' Macy said, 'are there any houses near by, or pubs?'

'He could have been murdered miles away and just dumped here,' Jo said and added, as she started to think it through, 'Mind you, someone might have seen the dumping.'

'Don't spend too long on it,' Macy said before he drove away, 'and don't worry, I'm not exactly going to have a nice afternoon either.'

'So what happened?' Alan said to Jo as they walked back to where the body had been found. When she didn't answer, he added, 'I suppose not everyone's got a strong stomach like me.' It was not an apology but it was said like one and Jo stopped glaring at him.

'I turned over the usual stones yesterday,' Alan rattled on, 'the Sally Army hadn't heard of him. I couldn't find anything on his car – but the police will find that soon enough. I don't see it here?'

'Apparently not. I heard one of the constables say there were no vehicles in the lay-by when the body was found.' Some of the police cars were leaving now and the scene around the lay-by was less hectic. There were no houses or buildings in sight. 'Just behind the woods is the reservoir, do you know it? I think there's a pub there – a new place. It can't be far away. I'll go there if you like.'

It was not just the easiest option, it was the only option, as Jo saw it. She didn't know of any houses near by and the pub was the only place she could think of that was in walking distance. Alan was quite happy to linger around the scene of the crime and meet her at his car in an hour. Jo watched him stomp off towards Sergeant Beatty. He had left his customary anorak at home because of the hot weather and was wearing a home-made cardigan and sandals. Sometimes she forgot how much she could dislike Alan. And this job.

Chapter Six

Jo couldn't bring herself to cut through Gollins Wood although she guessed it would be quicker. The sun was strong and the tarmac felt hot through her espadrilles, but she still preferred to go along the road. Anyway she didn't mind walking further: it cleared her thoughts.

She passed no buildings, just fields and hedges, and wondered what a Londoner like Sean Fitzpatrick was doing around here – dead or alive. So far his only definite connection with the area seemed to be the sports club – and civilized Leamington seemed miles away, although actually it was nearer than Coventry. She must go to that club and see what she could find out – that is, if Connor still wanted to know, Jo reminded herself.

She turned down the road signposted to Leamington and a glimpse of the reservoir in a slight dip on her left reassured her that this was the right way. Dozens of bright sails billowed to and fro on the sheen of the water, despite the calm day. Then she saw the pub ahead and started to look forward to a cold bottle of beer.

The Castaway had not been open very long: maybe five years. It was the kind of place you drove out to for Sunday lunch in the summer. Jo remembered sitting outside looking at the lake. Had she brought her mother here for lunch one Mother's Day? Yes, that was it. Her mother had said she couldn't eat anything because it was all Indian food.

There was a large car park in front of the pub, which

was almost empty. It was early for lunch-time customers. Inside the smell of last night's beer mingled with frying onions from the kitchens, where a radio was playing very faintly. A man behind the bar was idly stacking tokens for one of the games machines. He looked up when he saw Jo and picked up a tea towel in a business-like manner. 'Hello, what can I get you?'

Jo ordered her cold beer and turned to see the rest of the place. A huge glass window offered good views of the lake along the back of the room; the decor was very light and modern with cane chairs and pastel prints. Just this side of naff, Jo thought. Two or three of the window seats were occupied but there was no one else at the bar.

As she paid for her beer, she told the barman she was looking for someone. 'Apparently he comes in here,' Jo said, handing over Sean's photograph. 'Do you know him?' The big, moustached man behind the bar looked at it for a second and shook his head. Obviously a man of few words, Jo thought. 'Oh, that's a shame,' she said, not taking the photograph back straight away.

'Wait there a minute,' the barman said at last, 'I'll go and ask the boss.' He took the photograph into the white-tiled kitchen at the back.

The barman came back, bringing his boss: a short, serious Indian in a crisp blue shirt with the sleeves rolled up. He was looking at the photograph and at Jo. 'Hello. My name is Matti. How do you do. You know this man?'

There was something about his earnestness and air of authority that made Jo decide to lie as little as possible. After all, Sean's death would be big news soon enough. 'Well, I know his brother,' she explained, 'Sean Fitzpatrick – the man in the photo – has gone missing. His brother is trying to find him. I think he may have come in here?'

'Yes, I think so.' Matti still stared at the photograph. He placed it on the bar. 'Hold on, I'll get my brother, he does more serving than me.' He left to get reinforcements. The barman looked on, his hands wrapped around his tea towel. 'Sorry I can't help,' he said, when he caught Jo's eye, 'I only work lunchtimes. Never seen him meself. I'm sure of that.' He sounded sorry to be left out.

Matti came out of the kitchens with his brother, obviously younger, in a white kitchen overall. He came up to her eagerly. 'Let me see this photograph. I've a good memory for faces.' Jo handed it over silently and they all studied it. This is detection by committee, she thought, as she sipped her beer and waited.

'I've seen him.' Matti's younger brother spoke up. 'Not often. Maybe only once even but he's definitely been in here.'

Jo felt an unexpected rush of satisfaction. 'Can you remember when? How long ago, roughly?'

Matti's brother thought about it while the photograph was passed round again. 'In the last two months, because I've seen him since I came back from my holidays.'

'Shahm went to India in the Spring,' Matti explained.

'What about before then?' Jo asked. 'Did you see him before your holiday?'

'I don't think so.' Shahm shook his head. 'But I've definitely seen him since. He was quiet. A whisky drinker, I think, definitely shorts anyway.' He turned to his brother. 'Don't you remember? Someone rang the pub for him and I had to shout his name out – that doesn't often happen.'

'Can't you say for sure when this happened?' Jo asked.

'I really don't know. About a month or so ago maybe.'

'Was he on his own?'

Shahm frowned, clearly trying to be helpful. 'Sorry. But I do remember he was here: quite a tall bloke, isn't he? Not very friendly. I think it was early evening because we weren't busy. There was a call for him.' Shahm dipped his head towards the phone behind the bar. 'I called out his name and he came over—'

'Did you say anything to him about the call?' Matti

interrupted. 'We don't encourage customers to take calls here or the phone would be busy all the time,' he explained to Jo.

Shahm's smooth young face creased up in an effort to remember. 'I don't think I did,' he said slowly, 'I was going to but something stopped me. Maybe I was serving someone else. I think perhaps I didn't want to speak to him because he seemed so bad tempered.' Shahm avoided Matti's eyes and smiled at Jo. 'Why do you want to know all this?'

'He went missing on the eighteenth of June,' Jo answered carefully. 'I don't suppose you remember who rang him? Man? Woman?'

'Woman, I *think*, but—' Shahm shrugged. 'Look, I'll keep racking my brain about it. Maybe I'll remember something else.' He looked up at Jo from under long eyelashes. 'Why don't you stay for lunch? I'm cooking today and I'm a good cook—'

'Sorry, I can't, someone's waiting for me,' Jo said regretfully. 'But hold on to the photograph. One of your customers might recognize him. Let me know if they do.' She gave Shahm her business card and he promised earnestly that he would get in touch if anything else occurred to him.

Behind her a group of men had come in and the barman went off to serve them. They were all young, wearing shorts and had an overtly sporty look. Jo guessed they must be from the sailing club, which was not far away. She asked Matti if she could show them the photograph but they were no use. They giggled together and looked at it blankly. She asked them where the sailing club was and one of them pointed unhelpfully towards the lake.

'I might have guessed it was in that general direction,' Jo remarked before leaving by the door in the plate-glass window.

It was very warm outside. Jo looked at Draycote

Water, hazed and flat below. Really she ought to be starting back to meet Alan but she thought she would try to find the sailing club as it seemed to be the only other place where Sean could have been going to or coming from. A sign on a wooden fence reminded her she was on land owned by the water authority but a gate stood open and a gravelled path took her to the lakeside.

Despite all the boats on the water, there was nobody about. The reservoir was surrounded by marshy ground with a high concrete dam at one end. She found the clubhouse easily enough: a low structure that looked like it might fall down in a high wind. It had a bar upstairs that could be hired for birthday parties and other functions, if the posters were to be believed, but the building had a temporary look about it. There was no one about. Jo wandered around to the boat houses where the dinghies were kept. She saw locked sheds with boats, windsurfing boards and mountain bikes inside but nobody to speak to. If Connor wanted them to carry on with the case, she would have to come back for a more thorough look but now she had to go and meet Alan.

Jo walked back up to the road. She was puzzled that Sean had been at the Castaway. Apart from the Indian food and the nearby sailing club, it was nothing special. It was nowhere near any large settlement and it was not on a main road. Sean would have had to go out of his way to find it. And why would he do that?

When Jo reached the road Alan's ancient Austin was waiting for her. He had driven to meet her and when she got in she saw immediately that he was in a self-congratulatory mood. With his old-fashioned side-parting and his square glasses, he reminded her of a game show host fallen on hard times.

'We're a step ahead of the police, anyway,' he announced as he drove off. 'They wouldn't tell me a thing. Just that the bloke had been dead for over a week, which you'd already told me. So I went up the lane and started asking around.'

'I'm surprised there was anyone to ask,' Jo said when she could get a word in.

'There's a couple of houses and a farm towards Princethorpe. I've got a print of Fitzpatrick's picture so I waved it under the noses of the locals.'

'And?' Jo knew there was some news coming, and her patience with Alan soon wore thin.

'No one had seen or heard of him. But...' Alan paused to heighten the suspense, 'I had a long talk with the farmer. I told him what had happened and whereabouts. He said two weeks ago he saw a girl and a car in that lay-by. She was having some trouble with the car and she was there quite a while fixing it.'

As he seemed to have come to an end, Jo sighed: 'Is that it?'

'Well, yes. But he gave a very good description. It was an old blue Chevette: Y registration and a vinyl roof.'

'What about the woman?'

'Hmm? Oh, he didn't remember her so well. Just said she was tall and blonde and wearing a red and white jacket.'

'When was this?'

'About quarter to nine he reckons because he had just packed up for the day and was driving the tractor back across one of the fields about half a mile from the woods.'

'If it really was two weeks ago that would be handy because it's exactly two weeks today since Sean went missing.'

'That's right,' Alan said triumphantly. 'Coincidence or what?' He seemed most pleased because he had found out this information before the police. 'Just as I was coming away, two uniforms were going to the farm,' he chortled. 'I bet they hadn't been to the pub either. By the way, did you get anything there?'

'Yes, the barman – well, barboy really – recognized Sean's photograph and says he was there one night – but he couldn't remember exactly how long ago. Maybe two weeks or maybe more—'

Alan was longing to interrupt so he could begin an enthusiastic hypothesis but Jo stopped him. 'Listen, there's more. Sean received a phone call at the pub. The barman thinks it might have been a woman.'

'Right. I get it. Maybe Sean goes to the Castaway to meet the girl—'

'Yes, but why meet there? Why that pub?' Jo wanted to know.

Alan clearly didn't think this was worth dwelling on. 'God knows,' he said dismissively. 'What if he went there two weeks ago today to meet his girlfriend? Say she was the girl the farmer saw in the lay-by and she didn't turn up because her car had broken down.' Alan was getting so worked up his driving was suffering and he had to slam the brakes on at a red light. 'The girl gives Sean a ring to tell him. There's a phone box two hundred yards down the lane from the lay-by. I passed it.'

'Hold on—' Jo tried to interrupt but Alan had built up a head of steam and a mere Virgo was not going to stop an Arian in full flow. Jo bided her time.

'Then the poor bloke goes out to help her and gets a bang on the head for his trouble.' Alan went on, 'It's his judy who bumped him off. Must have been.'

'You're making it up as you go along,' Jo said patiently, ignoring Alan's sexist slang, which like his clothes seemed to be stuck in the 1950s. 'Mind you, Connor Fitzpatrick told me his brother had a new girlfriend called Rosie.'

'We'll have to trace her. Did you find anything out in London yesterday?'

'Nothing spectacular. His office think he's off sick. His mother didn't seem to care where he was.'

'This Rosie didn't crop up in any of the conversations, did she?' Alan asked hopefully. Jo shook her head but he went on undaunted, 'Still, at least I've got a description of the Chevette. I'll concentrate on tracing that because the bobbies will turn up Sean's car in no time.' He pulled into the car park near Macy's office. Even Jo, who had a long stride and walked quite fast herself, had trouble keeping up with his energetic pace. They stopped on the way, at her suggestion, for sandwiches. The peanut butter and banana ones she had bought yesterday had been substandard but there was a deli in the city centre which did them just the way Jo liked.

Celia said she expected Macy back any minute so Jo ate her sandwiches while Alan regaled them with his theory. Celia was impressed but Macy, when he arrived, was distinctly less enamoured of it. 'Absolute speculation,' he commented when Alan presented the open and shut case.

Alan was not put off his stride. 'You have to admit this Rosie woman is suspect number one,' he insisted.

'Do you have to speak in capital letters?' Macy sighed. 'Can't you see I've had a gruelling experience? I've just spent half the day in the mortuary.'

Jo decided to support Alan's theory just to be awkward. 'But we're fairly sure Sean was at the Castaway and he took a call. He must have gone off to meet her in the lay-by,' she pointed out in her most reasonable tones.

'Hold on.' Macy accepted coffee and a packet of cigarettes from Celia. He was half-lying in an armchair, and as he had most of his staff gathered round him, he was making the most of the dramatic possibilities. 'Point one: we don't know if this Rosie has anything to do with Coventry. Point two: the girl in the lay-by might not have been connected with Sean and, incidentally, I'm not sure a woman would have had sufficient strength to wallop him over the head. He was a big bloke—'

'We don't know but we can deduce,' Jo argued. 'I thought that was what detectives were meant to do.'

'We're not detectives, we're investigators,' Macy said pedantically. 'As I was saying. Point three: we don't even know if Sean Fitzpatrick died anywhere near Gollins Wood. His body could have been dumped there.'

'Don't smoke, it'll kill you,' Jo said smugly when he paused for a drag on his cigarette.

'I have to, I'm traumatized. I'm no good at comforting people.'

'Did Connor take it badly, then? Jo asked. She still felt unjustifiably suspicious of Connor.

'Pretty badly. The police had called him and he was on his way from London, accompanied by the Met, when I got to the station. I went with him to see the body. He's still with the police now as far as I know. I've offered to drive him back.'

'And he still wants us to keep the case?' Jo asked.

'Yes, that's the only bit of good news I've had all day.' Macy stared into his coffee cup thoughtfully. 'I rang Sergeant Beatty, by the way, and she had some information which supports your flimsy theory. Apparently Sean had not been robbed. He didn't have much cash on him but he still had all his credit cards – including his cheque card so it was probably him who made that cash withdrawal on the eighteenth.'

'And spent it by the time he died,' Jo pointed out. 'Sixty pounds, wasn't it? Anyway I think it's important that we find Rosie if that's who the girl in the lay-by is.'

'I'll put out some feelers about the car. I've got a few contacts in that department.' Alan looked knowing. 'Which reminds me. About your car—' He turned to Jo but Macy interrupted.

'All right,' he said, a gust of cigarette smoke signalling his defeat, 'follow up these leads but we do have something else to go on. I'm more interested in finding out about Fitzpatrick himself—'

'Sean or Connor?' Jo asked.

'Both, actually, but you've got a good opportunity to find out more about Sean. You've got an interview at his bank. They rang here this morning. Apparently you applied for a job? Well, you've been shortlisted. I said you would be there on Monday at ten o'clock.'

Jo accepted this calmly. An expenses-paid trip to London was not to be turned down out of hand but she failed to see what more she could find out of the bank. She thought it would be more useful to look for Rosie but the only possible lead in that direction was the blue Chevette. As Alan was going to follow that up and Macy was looking after Connor, she seemed to be superfluous once again.

'When do you want me to look at your car, Jo?' Alan asked, getting to his feet.

'As soon as you can. It's got worse. It's making a terminal clicking noise now and that's all I can get out of it,' Jo explained anxiously.

'Sounds like you've bought a pig in a poke to me.'

'Thank you, but it's your advice on the mechanics I'm after, not on my financial decisions,' she said acidly.

'All right, I'll come along and look at it now if you like,' he said amiably. That was one of the good things about Arians, Jo reflected. They could dish it out but they could take it too. During this exchange, Macy seemed to have forgotten they existed and was asking Celia if there was anything around for him to eat. Jo didn't like being ignored, however, so before she left the office she suggested that Macy should ask Connor a couple of questions. 'See if Sean liked sailing or Indian food,' she said enigmatically before she breezed out with Alan in tow.

Chapter Seven

Watching while Alan delved around in the Renault's engine, Jo realized why Macy put up with him. Rude and bigoted he might be but he was also reliable and competent. After half an hour or so, he declared the car needed a new solenoid and he could get one at trade price if she wanted.

When he had driven off to get it, Jo went inside, made herself a coffee and mentally reviewed her finances, which never seemed to be very healthy. Her recent savings had virtually all gone on buying and insuring the car and she realized she was going to have to do some more work for Macy to cover this unexpected expense.

Of course she would have preferred to rely on her astrology business to bring in the extra money but she was dependent on the orders coming in. She advertised in some of the New Age magazines and, less expensively, in local entertainment guides but the work still went in fits and starts. Just before Christmas she had been kept busy doing what really fascinated her: casting charts and progressing them to give some idea of future trends. But this work had dropped off lately.

She had a regular income from her weekly horoscope column, which she wrote for a local paper under the name of Giovanna Conti – she had borrowed her paternal grandmother's name because it sounded more interesting than Jo Hughes. Her weekly wage didn't quite pay the rent so for the moment she needed the PI work.

It could be worse. At least working for Macy wasn't boring – and he paid reasonably well. All the same, she must have been mad to think she could afford a car. She wandered out on to the fire escape and looked down at the little white Renault with feelings that were decidedly mixed. Even though she viewed it with distrust for letting her down, she couldn't sell it yet – it would be such an admission of defeat. Thank God Alan's labour was free, anyway.

Although Alan clearly thought it would be beyond Jo to understand, he did try to explain what he was doing when she asked. He virtually had to strip down the engine, which took him hours, and he eventually overcame his reluctance to ask her for help. Even so it took them all afternoon to get the starter motor working again. When Alan left, Jo just had time to get to the local shop to buy herself some dinner. Out of politeness she had asked Alan to stay but, as she had expected, he went home where she guessed his mother would have his tea warming in the oven.

As she put the key in the door of her flat, the phone was ringing. She hurried towards it, hampered by her carrier bag of shopping, and reached it just before the answering machine started up.

'Jo! It's Shahm!' came an excited voice down the line. 'You're in at last. You know, from the Castaway. You were in at lunch time asking about that Fitzpatrick bloke.'

'Oh yes. Hi.' Now that she had identified who was calling, she was unsurprised. Something about Shahm's attentive manner at lunch had told her that having been given her telephone number, he was likely to use it.

'I've got something for you. Some information—' Shahm sounded even younger than he had looked.

'About Sean Fitzpatrick?'

'Yes, but I can't tell you on the phone. I'm at the pub but I can get the evening off. Do you want to come for a drink?'

Jo couldn't believe that she had just heard someone actually say 'I can't tell you on the phone'. She didn't really want to go out with Shahm. She had planned to cook herself a meal for a change. She still had some work to do for Macy on checking the would-be nurses' references and she wanted to finish off Sean's chart. 'No, I'm sorry,' she said definitely, 'I haven't eaten all day and I'm going to cook myself a dinner and have a quiet night in.'

'Oh... I can cook something for you?' Shahm offered hopefully.

'That's nice of you, but no – honestly. Look, why can't you tell me this news now? My phone's not bugged, I promise.'

Shahm agreed reluctantly. 'I know now why you were asking questions at lunch time. About that customer. He's dead, isn't he? The police came round later.'

'Yes. It looks like he was murdered and his brother is paying us to find out more about it.'

'I thought a bit more about him and I'm sure I only saw him that once maybe two or three weeks ago. I asked some of the regulars who come in after work most nights. One of them remembered him as well.'

'Go on,' Jo said, sliding down the wall to sit on the floor beside her shopping.

'One of them is a guy called Ben – he's about the same age as me and works at the Jag. He lives not far away. He doesn't remember much about the man that died but he tried to chat up the girl he was with.'

'Fitzpatrick was with a woman?' Jo repeated. That puts paid to Alan's theory, she thought.

'Yes. Ben was chatting to her because she was sitting on her own and the place was virtually empty. This would be around seven, I think. She said her name was Rosie—'

'Definitely Rosie?'

'Yes, a pretty fair-haired girl with long legs, Ben said.' Shahm paused. 'I prefer dark girls myself,' he added significantly.

Jo laughed. 'Go on. Tell me more about this woman. Do you remember her?'

'No, I don't recall seeing her but I believe him. Why would he make it up? I didn't even tell him that Fitzpatrick had been murdered. I couldn't – the police asked us not to mention it to the customers just yet.'

'What else did he say about her? Does he remember the day?'

'Thinks it was a Friday about two weeks ago. He remembers this Rosie was quite friendly at first, said she was an actress. She said she was waiting for someone and Ben shouldn't hang around – that bit might have been just to get rid of him. But she was telling the truth because Ben remembers seeing her sitting with a guy later.' Shahm came to a halt. 'That's about it, really. Can you tell us anything about how this Fitzpatrick was killed? Did you see the body? Was it, like, really gory?'

'It was pretty horrible. It had been eaten by foxes and God knows what,' Jo told him, guessing this would go down well.

'I didn't know you got women private detectives,' Shahm confided, 'I didn't even know you got actual private detectives at all, to be honest. Outside the television, you know.'

They chatted for a while about the strange nature of her job and Shahm said he wanted to cook her a lamb korma, which was his speciality. Jo promised to call in at the Castaway sometime. She had no idea that when she did, she would be in no mood to enjoy Shahm's cooking.

Chapter Eight

Somewhat to Jo's surprise, the next morning the car started first time. She had been intending to walk into Coventry but she couldn't resist trying it out. Pleased with life – even pleased with Alan – Jo sat there for a few minutes grinning like an idiot and listening to the engine ticking away unconcernedly. As it was working, she decided, she might as well drive it into town – although she knew that taking a car into Coventry on a Saturday morning was good neither for the environment nor her patience. She ignored these thoughts, pulled the umbrella-handle gear lever into first and drove off, feeling decidedly cheerful.

Jo was not what you might call a patient driver. In common with many Virgos, her normally temperate and reasonable nature seemed to undergo a transformation when she was behind a steering-wheel. It was simply that when concentrating on driving, she forgot to conceal her innate belief that everyone apart from herself was totally incompetent, which she usually disguised very successfully. Finding herself behind a lorry festooned with bunting, slowly making its way to join the rest of the carnival procession, her good mood evaporated in seconds. She overtook it rashly on the only bend in the Kenilworth Road, provoking an outraged flash of headlights from an innocent Ford Fiesta coming the other way.

By the time she arrived at the Belgrade Theatre, she felt irritable, grimy and sweaty. She caught sight of her flushed face, glaring back at her from the rear-view mirror. Her hair was already looking disordered. She pushed back some curly strands from her eyes and brought her mind to bear on the subject in hand. If Sean's girlfriend Rosie was an actress, the most obvious place to look for her was the Belgrade, which was the only professional theatre in Coventry.

She read the car parking charges, looked round but couldn't see any traffic wardens and decided to risk not paying. The stage door near where she was parked was closed and locked so she strolled round to the front of the theatre. It looked a plain, no-fuss building. The sparkle of lights through the plate-glass gave the only hint of a more lavish interior. The coffee bar near the door was busy and, hearing the sound of fractious babies from inside, Jo hurried past towards the box office, which was simply a large desk in the foyer. The middle-aged lady behind it regarded Jo suspiciously before denying any knowledge of an actress called Rosie. 'We haven't got a permanent company here,' she added. 'Why do you want to know?'

Jo blithely produced her prepared story. 'She came to a party at my flat and left her coat behind. I thought I should try to find her but all I really know is that she's an actress and I thought she must work somewhere in Coventry – or near by.'

The woman behind the desk pursed her lips and looked into the distance to indicate she was giving the matter some serious thought. 'There are quite a few amateur theatre companies in the area,' she said, as if she was admitting something distasteful like having to offer the use of an outside toilet. 'But if your friend said she was an *actress* that does imply that it's her *job*, doesn't it?'

'That's what I thought,' Jo said encouragingly. 'Any ideas about where else I could try?'

The other woman seemed to shed her suspicions and accept Jo's question as a way to pass the time on a slow morning. 'Well, there's the Arts Centre at the University but they tend to have very short runs – a week at most. When was your party?'

'Two weeks ago. June the eighteenth, actually.'

'You see, if she had been working here then she would have moved on by now. So you'll have to look further afield. In Birmingham there's the Rep, the Hippodrome and the Alex – you'd need to find out what was playing on the eighteenth to see if she's still around. Ring up the theatres, they'll probably send you cast lists if you ask nicely.'

Behind Jo, a family had arrived to buy some tickets, so she moved aside and thanked the woman for her help.

'You might try the Spa Centre at Leamington,' the woman added before turning to her customers. 'They've got a variety show that's been running all summer. It's not *acting*, of course, but...' She followed this up with a look which finished the sentence.

The day was getting warmer and some people were sitting in the square outside the theatre. Kids were leaning over the side of the fountain, threatening to fall in, as Jo walked past. She didn't fancy having to trek round the many theatres in Birmingham: it would be easier to call them up, Jo thought, making her way back to the car. But the Spa Centre at Leamington wasn't far away and the idea of a jaunt there appealed. At the same time, she could have a look at Greenaways Lifestyle Club, the membership card for which was still in her handbag. Macy had shown no interest in it but she was convinced it was worth following up.

She lost her way in Leamington trying a short cut that worked perfectly well on foot, but she eventually found her way to the Parade, which was busy with Saturday shoppers. Jo was watching out for the more suicidal ones and almost missed her turning up one of the wide shady roads. She braked sharply and turned left. The man in the car behind hooted, which she considered to be an emotional over-reaction. There was a big space in the row of imposing white houses, like a gap tooth. This was the concrete arena in front of the Spa Centre. Jo knew it well because she often went to see films there.

Parking was easy, but when Jo walked over to the theatre she saw it had a distinctly closed look about it. A Summer Special was advertised, just as the woman in the Belgrade box office had said, but unlike the Belgrade, there seemed to be nowhere to buy tickets for it. She went round the back but the place seemed to be completely closed and there was no one around to ask when it might be open.

Jo had imagined that finding an actress in a relatively small city like Coventry would be easy. Now it seemed she would have to phone round the theatres in Birmingham and any other places to which theatre companies had taken themselves since the middle of June. But she was convinced it was worth pursuing. If this blonde woman had seen Sean on the night he died, she must be important, she thought again as she got back in the car. She was also convinced that Rosie must be Sean's reason for coming to this area. She had yet to come up with any other explanation.

Maybe the Greenaways Club could provide another. As it was only a short distance away, according to the street map, she went on foot and walked past the place by mistake. Greenaways was nothing if not discreet. Retracing her steps, she noticed the brass plaque beside the sober Prussian blue front door. She walked up the steps, which were bounded by a graceful iron balustrade, pushed the bell and waited. She guessed a Lifestyle Club would be a smart version of the Sports Centre in Coventry but this place looked more like solicitors' or architects' offices.

'Good afternoon,' came a sexless voice through a speaker, and Jo asked if she could come inside.

There was a long pause before she was buzzed in,

during which she noticed a camera lens peering through the ivy foliage. This made her even more curious but once inside, the place was innocuous enough. She stepped into a wide lobby with black and white tiles on the floor and six-foot-high palms and fig trees grouped in the corners. At the back of the lobby two women in identical green track suits were talking quietly over a curved wooden desk.

The woman with her back to Jo threw a look over her shoulder and said, 'I might be back this evening, Jane. I've got some more practice to do. Bye.' She picked up a sports holdall and walked past Jo on the way to the front door. The green track suits made them look a bit like extras from *Star Trek*, Jo thought.

Jane, the receptionist, turned to her enquiringly. She was tall – a head taller than Jo – and had wide athletic shoulders and short, tidy curly hair.

'I'm thinking of becoming a member,' Jo said, 'can you give me any details about the club?'

'I can give you a brochure,' Jane said, handing over a glossy pamphlet. By her accent she was Australian. 'But I can't do much else because today is a man's day. We have single-sex days twice a week. It makes people feel more relaxed.'

'You see, I'm looking for a club that has very extensive facilities – gyms, pools, weights, that sort of thing,' Jo said vaguely to keep the conversation going.

'Perhaps you could give the club a ring after you've read the brochure. But we do have a long waiting list for membership.' Jane was polite but unsmiling.

'That's a shame. I particularly wanted to join this club. It was recommended to me by a friend,' Jo continued, pretending she was the kind of insensitive soul who didn't recognize the end of a conversation when she heard it. 'His name's Sean Fitzpatrick. Do you know him?'

'Not off-hand. Is he a member?'

Jo produced the plastic card. 'I think so. He gave me this.'

Jane glanced at it. 'That's only a day ticket, not a full membership card. He must have spent a day here once.'

Jo did not have to call on her acting skills to sound disappointed. 'Oh, I'm sure he told me he was a member. Is there any way you can check?'

'Yes, but there's no need.' Jane was pleasant but assertive. 'I can tell he's not a member from that card.'

'But he's probably got a membership card as well,' Jo said logically.

The other woman sighed and tapped the keyboard in front of her, frowning. 'No, he's not on here,' she announced with some satisfaction. 'We don't keep a list of day visitors – only members.'

By leaning over the low desk, Jo could see the computer screen reading *no records found*. 'Thank you anyway,' she said, 'I wonder why he said he was. I'll think about joining myself.' She moved away from the desk and Jane smiled politely.

'By the way,' Jo added as an afterthought, 'you don't know anyone called Rosie, do you?'

Jane looked bemused. 'Yes, I know a few girls called Rosie and one puppy dog, but what does that have to do with the price of bacon?'

Jo grinned. 'Another friend. A friend of Sean's too, as a matter of fact. I don't know her surname—'

'Well, I'm not searching our records for all the Rosies,' Jane said decidedly. 'Did this Rosie say she was a member too? Because if it's any help, I can't think of any members with that name so your friends may be telling you porkies. There is someone but she works here—'

'A Rosie who works here?' Jo took a step forward again. 'Is she here now?'

'No. She's only part time. Look, what is this all about?' Jane sounded more puzzled than irritated.

'Well, I suddenly remembered Sean said a girl called Rosie recommended this place to him. I just wondered if she was around—'

'She's just left. In fact she passed you on the way out.'

Jo looked round automatically as if the woman with the hold-all would magically reappear. She had hardly noticed her and could only recall that she was tall and fair. 'When will she be back?'

'Maybe tonight. She uses the studio on the top floor to practise in. She's a dancer. Just works here mornings – but not tomorrow,' Jane added. 'She doesn't work Sundays.'

'Thanks. I might pop in and see her some time,' Jo said vaguely.

She left the club with mixed feelings. It was impossible to know if Rosie the dancer was the same as Rosie the actress who had been in the Castaway. And she wouldn't be able to call back at Greenaways on Monday morning because she would be at the bank being interviewed. She would just have to tell Macy and if he thought it was important enough, no doubt he would send Alan. She seemed to be doing all the legwork and missing all the fun with this case so far.

Back in the car, she glanced through the brochure, which boasted excellent sports facilities and an exorbitant membership fee. She stuffed it into her glove compartment, which she had already filled with any maps and guide books she could find, and decided to drive to see her sister. As Marie had not seen the car, Jo felt it was her sisterly duty to go and show it off.

Marie was married with two small sons, who made a very gratifying audience. Jo's nephews asked to be taken for a ride so she took them to see the ducks in the park. Afterwards, tired out by their current craze for piggybacks, Jo was easily persuaded to stay for dinner because Marie's cooking was not lightly refused. But it meant that by the time she drove back to the centre of Leamington it was nine o'clock and beginning to get dark. Instead of driving straight back to her flat, she couldn't resist going past Greenaways again.

Chapter Nine

Jo parked outside Greenaways and looked up at the double-fronted building. Downstairs the windows were long and elegant, their height decreasing with each floor. The white stucco was flawless, the hanging baskets dripped on to the painted wrought iron around the stairs and basement. The place was prosperous and well looked after.

There were lights on the top floor. Hadn't Jane said the dance studio was up there? Jo stared up and wondered if Rosie had come back to practise, as she said she would. She tried the front door bell but there was no answer. She took out Sean Fitzpatrick's membership card and swiped it across the slot below the microphone but the door didn't open.

She walked back down the steps and looked up at the building again. There were no cars outside, so if Rosie or anyone else was in there, where had they parked? Perhaps there was another entrance round the back. She turned the corner and walked along a little way. She knew these Regency houses usually had access at the back. Sure enough, there was a dark, wide stone-flagged alley running behind the row of houses. Jo wanted to get more of an idea what went on at Greenaways and so she walked down it, looking up at the houses on her right, the subtle scent of privet reaching her from the walled gardens.

Greenaways was the third one along. It had large

wooden doors wide enough to get a car through. Both were closed. She tried one of them and it opened. She stepped into a paved yard. One tree threw darkness in one corner. Across the yard were bins and basement steps and above that french windows leading on to a veranda. There was no sign of what went on inside or of any life until Jo heard the quick patter of footsteps from the side of the house.

It took one frozen second for her to realize what the sound actually was. Then the dog appeared. Waist high, black and running. It didn't bark and she could hear its claws on the cobbles and the jingle of its collar. She could see its teeth as it ran at her.

From somewhere in the depths of her mind she dragged up advice on confronting dogs. Don't run, she said to herself. In fact her feet felt immovable. She knew she should have shouted as well but couldn't summon any sound. The dog came within snapping distance and stopped. It had a blunt head and wet yellow teeth. It shifted its weight and rolled its head as if it wanted to come at her but was restrained by an invisible leash.

Jo's neck was rigid with fear. Her muscles had turned to chains which rooted her to the spot. Then the dog barked. The blast of sound and hot breath terrified her and she leapt back. Its head was near her armpit. She smelt the heat of the dog. It barked again, bellowing deep and loud, and bounded forward. She couldn't stop herself jumping back and then, against all sense, she tried to back up fast, stumbling. The dog caught her jacket in its mouth.

Jo felt the grip of the dog's teeth. She kept moving back, her eyes on the gate, and at the same time tried to struggle out of her jacket. The she felt a force like a truncheon blow on her arm and shoulder and she went down. Her face hit blue paving with the barking loud in her ears. The dog must be standing on her back.

The shout, when it came, was very loud, harsh and

unmistakably authoritative. Instantly Jo felt the dog stiffen and hesitate. She lay very still, the ground cold and gritty beneath her. The shout came again and the dog's weight moved off her. Jo couldn't understand what the person was shouting and didn't care. It worked. Above her there was scuffling, scraping of claws on paving, subdued growling and muttered commands.

Then a woman's voice said firmly, 'You can get up now.' Jo realized she had her eyes closed. She opened them. There was the blue paving. She sat up slowly. Her left side felt jarred. She was looking at sling-back sandals so white they seemed to glow in the dark, painted toenails and brown shiny legs. The dog was still there but held by the woman, who was wearing shorts and looking down at her with a mixture of wariness and disgust. Jo still didn't care. She mainly felt grateful. She could feel herself shaking and couldn't seem to say anything.

'Who in God's name are you?' The woman had a strong northern accent. From Jo's angle it seemed to come from a round doll's face, framed with pale wavy hair. 'What are you doing in the yard?'

'I couldn't get in the front way,' Jo managed finally. It was beyond her ingenuity just then to make up a story but she began working on one as she got gingerly to her feet, her eyes on the dog. It growled louder but the woman had her fingers in its collar and the other hand holding a chain lead.

'I'm not surprised,' the woman said crisply, 'we don't let just anybody in.'

Jo saw them in perspective now. The dog was a Dobermann, brown and black with massive paws, and its head came up to the woman's elbow. She was small and neat and frowning. Jewellery glittered on her fingers and throat.

Jo hunted up a good reason for trespassing. 'I was meeting Rosie. She said to come round the back if the front door was locked,' Jo said in desperation. Examining herself for damage, she noticed that her expensive denim jacket was torn and wondered if she could sue.

'Rosie left half an hour ago,' the other woman said shortly. 'I'll have to have a word with her about arranging to meet friends here. It's not on.' She stared at Jo in obvious annoyance before she added, 'I'm sorry about the dog, but Rupert was only doing his job. I suppose you'd better come in for a minute if you've hurt yourself.'

Jo looked down at her knee and saw blood. Until then she had only been aware of a stinging sensation but suddenly it hurt and her face felt sore too.

'I'll put Rupert away and clean that up for you.' The smaller woman led the dog, still held close, back up the yard and Jo followed slowly behind. It was somehow irritating to have been attacked by a dog called Rupert. She decided that when she recounted this incident to Macy the dog would have to be re-named Mugger, Slugger or Bugger. She stopped a hysterical giggle before it could get a hold and watched with some satisfaction as Rupert was shunted unceremoniously into a small modern conservatory. Once shut in, he calmly went and lay down on a mat.

Jo felt her breath coming more easily now there was glass between her and the dog. But it still took a bit of courage to walk past it to where the woman was holding the back door open. Jo went through into a kitchen which was almost as spruce and clean-looking as the woman herself.

'Sit down and I'll get you some tea,' she ordered. Jo sat by a white marble breakfast bar while the woman briskly filled the kettle and set out two mugs. Jo couldn't imagine anything as untidy as cooking going on in such a kitchen.

A first-aid box was produced and the woman sorted through it to find what she wanted. Her tanned hands were deft, all her movements quick and practical, her lips pursed. In fact she reminded Jo of a nurse but her perfume was too strong and her lip gloss too shiny. Jo watched as antiseptic was poured and mixed with warm water.

'That was a bit stupid, trying to get in round the back, you know. But Rosie knows about the dog. She's a very silly girl, telling you to meet her there. And then not waiting for you.'

Jo felt a pang of guilt as her story had clearly landed Rosie in it. Still, Rosie only had to deny all knowledge of her and all, presumably, would be well. She wondered what would happen if this woman ever looked at the videotapes of today's visitors, in which Jo no doubt featured. There was no use worrying about that now though.

'Actually I'm interested in joining the club. Do you run it?' Jo asked. She accepted a mug of strong sugared tea, which she normally would have poured away.

'Yes. I'm Kelly Greenaway,' the doll-faced woman said, smiling suddenly. Jo put down her mug to shake the small hand. 'If you really want to join, I'll just do your knee and then I'll show you round if you like,' she said, bending down to examine the cut. 'Almost everyone's gone home now but me, I virtually live here – as my husband is always saying – so another few minutes won't make any difference.' She swabbed Jo's knee with cotton wool soaked in the antiseptic solution.

'Thank you. That would be nice,' Jo said faintly. The cut was not a dog bite, as she had first thought, but a bad graze where she had fallen. Other injuries amounted to a very sore left side and what felt like a slight cut on her face.

'I feel bad that a member of my staff was so irresponsible. Mind you, it's typical of Rosie to forget about the dog and the arrangement. She's wrapped up in herself.' Kelly's ministrations were brief and to the point and Jo was feeling better by the time she had finished the tea.

'If you leave your jacket here, I'll have it mended,' Kelly said airily, packing up the first-aid box. 'There's a wonderful old-fashioned tailor in town who does all sorts of alterations. Being short I'm always going there to have my dresses and trousers taken up.' Kelly smiled again and the atmosphere between the two women seemed to become a degree warmer.

Jo agreed to leave the jacket although she thought Kelly was being over-generous. If she tried to sew it herself, she knew it would never look wearable. Feeling that she might as well find out everything she could about the place now that she had been to all this trouble, Jo asked Kelly if she really would show her round.

'Of course, if your knee's not too stiff for a little walk. I'd put a plaster on it but I think a graze like that is best left to the air.'

'I'm fine,' Jo assured her and it wasn't until she got off the stool that she felt how painful her shoulder was. She touched it experimentally as she followed Kelly out of the kitchen.

'I love showing people round,' she admitted as she steered Jo towards a door on one side of a wide corridor. 'I don't often get the chance. I'm usually in the office. We'll start with the gym.'

She opened the door to a high-ceilinged room, which would probably have been the sitting-room of the house when it was built. She flicked the lights on to reveal a white-painted gym with mirrors down one wall and ten or twelve pieces of equipment, some linked to computers.

'This is one of our two fitness centres,' Kelly Greenaway announced, looking round as if she was seeing it for the first time herself. 'The equipment is the most sophisticated you will find. Are you interested in any form of exercise in particular?'

'No,' Jo said honestly. 'I swim regularly—'

'Absolutely the best thing for you.' Kelly nodded enthusiastically as they crossed the dim, echoing foyer, which held an oval reception desk. The room on the opposite side was almost identical except it contained mainly weight-training equipment. Jo thought that if the place hadn't looked so hygienically clean, it could have passed for a medieval torture chamber.

'I'll show you the pool next, then. We've got a sauna, plunge pool and a hot spa as well as sunbeds down there. You look pretty fit already, to be honest.' Kelly threw a long backward glance at Jo as they went down some stairs. 'Do you just want to keep in shape?'

The pool was about a quarter of the size of the public one she was used to in Coventry but it looked invitingly tranquil. 'Yes. Well, I do a sedentary job so I don't get much exercise,' Jo answered, her voice bouncing off the tiles.

'What do you do?' Kelly asked. She walked around the pool to tidy up some flotation aids that were lying around. Jo wondered if it was a strain to run a place like this and have to be a walking advertisement. Kelly's figure was not marvellous: she was too much of a classic English pear shape. But she did look good. Jo reckoned she was about five years older than herself – that would make her just in her thirties. Her hair was expensively bleached blonde and she had a tan – due to the sunbeds, no doubt.

'I'm an astrologer,' Jo said, deciding to tell part of the truth.

Kelly looked up, her pencilled eyebrows raised. 'Really? I'm fascinated with it myself. Do you do consultations? I've had my birth chart done but I'd love someone to explain it to me. It's one of those computerized ones and I don't understand all of it, to be honest. Are they any good?'

'Most people use computers to do the calculations,' Jo explained as they went back upstairs, 'but even the really good programmes can't interpret the chart. I could help you with that—'

'Yes, I would like that,' Kelly said warmly. There were squash and badminton courts for Jo to admire on the first floor as well as changing rooms, lockers and showers. 'I'm Aquarius, you know. Too scatty to be a business woman really,' she laughed.

Jo was never very sure about Aquarians. No sooner did she think she had them pinned down, than she met one who bore no relation to the others. One thing was certain, though: Kelly was not the airhead she appeared. There was probably a cool, shrewd brain beneath the synthetic exterior. 'It depends on the rest of your chart,' Jo said. 'Anyway Aquarians can usually manage to be more than one person at a time.'

'That's very true,' Kelly agreed, becoming more animated, 'when I'm at home with Mark I like being half-baked, it's relaxing, and when I'm here I become all assertive. I'm different again with Nina, that's my daughter. I have to be in control then – she's only three. This is our dance studio by the way.'

Rosie – or whoever had been there last – had left the lights on in the deserted studio and Kelly flicked them off one by one. 'Well, what do you think of the place?'

Jo made appreciative noises as they went back downstairs. In fact she was quite impressed but she knew she could never afford membership. In her pocket she had been holding Sean Fitzpatrick's membership card. She was determined to get him into the conversation somehow and took her chance when Kelly presented her with the opportunity.

'Did anyone recommend this place?' she asked as they hesitated in the foyer, 'or did you just see it advertised in the paper?'

Jo turned to look at Kelly. 'I heard about it from a friend. Sean Fitzpatrick. Do you know him?'

Kelly didn't answer straight away. She seemed to give the question some thought then said dismissively. 'No. Is he a member?'

Jo shook her head. She didn't see the point in getting Kelly to check the computer again. 'I don't think so. But he used to go on about this place. I haven't seen him for a while. Rosie knows him too,' she added with an inspired touch as she followed Kelly downstairs.

'Does she?' Kelly sounded vague and uninterested. They had reached the reception area and Jo glanced over at the brochures stacked neatly on the desk, the blotter and pens and blank computer screen with a box of disks beside it. Alongside the closed circuit TV screen was a stack of videotapes.

'Now you will think about joining yourself, won't you? And are you serious about looking at my birth chart?' Kelly was saying.

'Yes, send it to me and once I've interpreted it I'll bring it over and explain it,' Jo said enthusiastically. She was careful to hand over the card with her home number on, which she used for her astrology work, rather than the card from Macy and Wilson.

'You can tell me about it when you come and pick up your jacket,' Kelly suggested and this arrangement seemed to suit them both.

Jo left Greenaways feeling philosophical. OK, so she hadn't found out any more about Sean Fitzpatrick, she thought as she drove home. And she was nowhere nearer knowing whether the Rosie who worked there was his girlfriend. But she did have some valuable new astrology business and Kelly, who looked like a bimbo but acted like a shrewd businesswoman, might be an interesting subject. Jo wouldn't have minded being a member of her smart club. Maybe after a few more consultations among Kelly's rich friends, she might be able to afford it!

At the moment all she really wanted to do was to climb into a hot bath and feel sorry for herself. This small achievement was easily accomplished but as she stretched her aching side in the warm water there was one niggling little thought, which wouldn't go away. She was sure she had seen Kelly somewhere before but she couldn't place where.

Chapter Ten

Jo had been brought up to believe that those who had cars washed them on Sundays. As she now had one herself, her first thought on Sunday morning – despite her aches and pains – was to wash it. She woke up early after a poor night's sleep. She hadn't exactly had nightmares but she had woken up thinking about the dog's attack a few times.

After a coffee in bed, she examined herself in the tall bedroom mirror. Her left side felt worse but her other injuries were only grazes. Going up to the mirror, she studied the scratches on her face. Her grey eyes looked pretty much the same as usual – not black and swollen as she had half-feared. She hoped the cuts left by the gravel wouldn't bruise.

Washing the car seemed a good antidote for the vaguely anxious feelings left behind from yesterday. So she walked down to the local shop, which sold sachets of car cleaner that promised to wax at the same time as washing. She found a bucket under the sink, filled it with warm soapy water as directed and carried it carefully down the fire escape using her right arm. She didn't imagine for a moment that washing the car would become a regular weekly habit but she thought she might as well start off the right way.

The car was parked on the tarmac at the back of the old Victorian house in which Jo's flat was on the top floor. Although it was about ten o'clock by the time she got started, it felt like early morning. None of the other residents were about, the sun was hazy and the birds sang loud and undisturbed in the gardens near by. She was at the rinsing stage when Macy strolled round the corner of the house.

'How suburban of you,' he commented when he saw her. 'I tried the front door but there was no answer so I thought you might be out here.'

'I can see how you got to be where you are today.' Using her good arm, Jo threw the bucket of water at the car and Macy took a nervous step back. In his jeans and his cream shirt with his sunglasses dangling from the pocket, he looked at his best. Jo took this in, while appearing to concentrate on where exactly to throw the next bucket of clean water.

'How did you hurt your face?' Macy asked, leaning across the bonnet so he could see her properly.

Jo told him as briefly as possible, not wanting to dwell on the subject. Macy didn't say much. He told her the scratch on her face was only noticeable to a trained observer like himself.

'I thought I might get a black eye. How would that go down at my interview at the bank tomorrow?' She gave a laugh at the thought of it. 'I'm sure I'm going to be imagining all dogs are out to get me from now on.'

'Even Chihuahuas?' Macy asked lightly. He stepped away from the car to consider it critically. 'So this is it? I can see I don't have to accuse you of choosing a car to boost your image.'

'I don't have to worry that my choice of car says something about the size of my penis, as men do,' Jo remarked. That was proof she was feeling randy, she thought, because that word had suddenly appeared in her head from nowhere. Her aches couldn't be too bad after all.

'Just as well or your decision-making would have been an even more agonized process,' Macy responded, looking more at ease now the last bucket of water had been despatched. 'Do you want to take me out in it, then? Prove that it goes?'

'All right, come in for a drink while I get changed.' Jo was conscious that the way she looked in her wet and ancient dungarees was far from glamorous. She gave Macy a beer and left him in the deck chair with the Sunday paper while she went to put on a summer dress, which made her feel less like a grubby mechanic.

'Have the police turned up anything yet?' she asked when she rejoined him on the landing of the fire escape.

Macy looked up from the sports page. 'They've got the weapon, a wooden hammer – could be a croquet mallet—'

'Ah, a classy murder. Sorry, go on.'

'It was in the woods not far from the body. According to Debbie they've been trying to trace witnesses—'

'Debbie?'

'Sergeant Beatty,' Macy answered blandly. 'She says they haven't got very far with that. Apparently they've found the blue Chevette that the farmer saw parked in the lay-by. It was abandoned in a lane the other side of Princethorpe. It's a bit of an old banger and might not have anything to do with the case.'

'Who owns it?'

Macy shook his head. 'It's not registered but Debbie gave me the registration and I've passed it on to Alan. He reckons if it was sold in Coventry, he'll know who by and who to in no time—'

'Yes, he would say that, but he also said the police would find Sean's car first.'

'No. No news about that.' Macy folded up the paper. 'I've been thinking about Sean Fitzpatrick. We don't know much about him really, do we? What did he do when he wasn't at work? What sort of person was he? Have you any idea?'

After the routine exchange of insults, Macy and Jo had

returned to the only other kind of conversation they were relaxed with: work. Jo picked up her car keys and locked the back door of the flat. 'According to his chart, he's the kind of person who didn't have much of a life outside work. Earning money was very important to him.' She led the way down the fire escape. 'He liked a bit of excitement too. I don't think I'd have liked him much: he was too volatile and self-centred. He was bright, there's no doubt about that, but devious. An unusual Taurean.' Her work on Sean's chart was virtually finished and revealed a strong but flawed character. She had written it up as positively as she could to present to Connor but it had not been an easy job. 'Where shall we go?' she asked as she settled behind the wheel.

'A round-the-world trip, judging by the amount of maps you've got,' Macy said, peering into the glove compartment. 'As long as we're prepared to travel at seventy miles an hour, of course.' Jo glared at him and he added quickly, 'What about Stratford? We can feed the ducks with this old sandwich I've just found in here.'

'Oh, yes, I remember that one. I didn't like the bread, it tasted rubbery.'

It was not until they were bowling along the bypass that it occurred to Jo why Stratford was a particularly good place to visit. 'Of course, Stratford! I can carry on looking for Rosie there.' She turned her head to glance at Macy. 'What's at Stratford?' she demanded.

He sighed. 'Ducks,' he suggested.

'What else?'

'Tourists. Expensive restaurants. I don't know,' he said belligerently. Macy hated games like this. He was really no fun at all, Jo thought.

'Only one of the most famous theatres in the country,' she said sweetly.

'I'm not going to one of those long Shakespeare plays,' Macy said quickly, 'I'm only interested in the ducks—'

'No, no.' Jo was patient. 'I've been looking for theatres and I forgot the Royal Shakespeare, which is virtually on our doorstep, and so did the woman at the Belgrade.' She didn't know if Macy was keeping up with this but she carried on anyway. 'You know I've been trying to trace Rosie, who was with Sean in the pub the night he died—'

'The night we think he died,' Macy put in.

'Yes, June the eighteenth. The woman he was with that night was an actress and her name was Rosie. She got to the pub before him and left before him and then he got a call. The next thing we know is a woman's car broke down in that lay-by and his body is found near by. Well, I've been trying to trace her. There's a Rosie who works at Greenaways but I didn't get a chance to meet her. Anyway the woman in the pub said she was an actress—'

'And you forgot Stratford, which is probably the only theatre for miles which is still running the same play now as on June the eighteenth.'

Sometimes Macy surprised her, Jo had to admit. Mind you, it was easy for him to be clever once she had done the hard work.

'I take back what I said about this car only doing seventy,' Macy murmured as Jo sped along in the fast lane of the A46.

Jo dismissed this with a careless wave of her hand. 'I like going fast. Don't worry, you're quite safe.' In Stratford High Street she had to honk her horn at an ill-behaved coach and neatly cut up a Belgian car in order to park near the river.

'What do you make of the brother? Connor?' Macy asked as they walked past the church gates, where the shade was deep enough to make Jo shiver.

'You don't like him, do you?' she said.

'Can you think of anyone I do like?' Macy demanded. 'Liking has nothing to do with it. I don't *believe* him.'

They reached the river bank and looked at the packed pleasure boats narrowly missing the rowers. Macy took the aged sandwich out of its plastic bag and began to break it up for the ducks, who crowded round, greedy and satisfyingly grateful. 'Another thing that doesn't fit your picture of Sean is his financial difficulties,' he added. 'If he was a diligent bank clerk like you make out, why was he so badly in debt?'

'He was a bit more senior than a clerk,' Jo had to point out. 'Anyway I only know he owed Connor money. I must owe my sister money. It's not the same as being in debt.'

'Well, he was,' Macy said definitely. 'Sorry, that's all there is,' he added to the ducks. He turned to walk beside the river and Jo walked behind him, having to strain to hear what he said as his soft voice did not carry very well. 'Connor told me after he saw the body. He said he didn't know how bad Sean's debts were but it is in the thousands—'

'He probably gambled it away,' Jo suggested. 'After all, a middle manager's salary from the bank wouldn't go far if you spent most of your nights at casinos. Did you find out anything from those clubs?'

'I made a start. I swallowed my pride and went to see my ex-father-in-law. He runs Diamonds.'

Jo had once spent a boring evening at Diamonds, one of Coventry's few casinos. She filed away for future reference the fact that Macy must have married the daughter of its owner.

'George knew Sean Fitzpatrick,' Macy was saying, 'he wasn't exactly a regular but he'd been in now and then. Spent a lot and lost a lot. I'll go to the London ones next week. Knowing George is like a letter of introduction.'

They threaded between the clumps of tourists, who seemed to have a uniform of pale jackets, nylon trousers and either a camera dangling from their wrists or a folded square of map in their hands. Some had both. It was busier as they came closer to the town centre and the brick-built theatre jutting out across the river. Jo pulled Macy across the grass towards the Swan Theatre.

'There's another thing.' Macy, with his hands in his jeans pockets, was obviously more concerned with the disorder in his head than around him. 'Don't you think that Connor is more than a bit edgy?'

'Edgy? Yes, I noticed he seemed nervous when I went to his house.' Jo walked up the steps of the Swan, a separate theatre tacked seamlessly on to the back of the Royal Shakespeare. 'Come on, I want to go in here.'

They walked into an old-fashioned theatre lobby. The tourists had not neglected the Swan altogether but they were crowded into the small shop, which Jo ignored. With Macy following, she went through the doors and up to a counter. A girl in a baggy jumper smiled at them pleasantly. Jo asked if she had a cast list for the musical that was currently playing.

'Yes, hang on. I do have some.' She ducked down behind the counter for a moment and reappeared with a flyer. Jo scanned it briefly.

'It's just that I'm looking for a friend called Rosie. She said she worked here. Do you know her?'

The girl pulled at the sleeve of her jumper thoughtfully. 'I don't think I do,' she said regretfully. 'Sorry. Have you tried the main house? They'll give you cast lists for their productions.'

Jo and Macy retreated into the sunshine. A crowd of Japanese girls swarming around the steps pounced on Macy and asked if he would take a picture of them. Jo watched amused as he tried to get them to stand still while her mind went over the Rosie problem. She was not getting anywhere at present. Perhaps that was understandable. If the woman was Sean's murderess, would she really have offered her correct name and occupation to any oik who tried to chat her up?

'One more try,' she sighed. She led Macy round to the

front of the main theatre and through the spacious modern foyer. Macy looked around suspiciously as if someone might try to make him sit through three hours of *Henry IV Part Two* if he wasn't careful. Jo repeated her questions at the box office, where the staff were more numerous and less patient. There was no queue behind her so she stood where she was while she read through the three cast lists she had been given. The woman at the window watched her for a minute and then walked off through a door at the back of the box office. There was a Rosalind in *Romeo and Juliet* and Jo looked up hopefully.

'Excuse me,' she said, seeing she had been deserted. She repeated herself a few times until a young girl from another window came over and asked politely what she wanted. Jo began a complicated question and then stopped and stared at the girl in front of her. She had one of those faces which show a lot of skin: a broad face with hair scraped back from the forehead and wide, flat cheeks. Attractive but not pretty. Jo's eyes moved back to the badge on the girl's sweatshirt. *RSC Stratford*, it said, *Rosie Martell*.

'Are you Rosie?' Jo asked, trying desperately to remember if this was the woman who had passed her in Greenaways yesterday. It could be but she wasn't sure.

'Yes,' the girl answered, puzzled but not bothered.

'I've been looking for you. Is there any way we can have a word?'

'Looking for me? What do you mean?' Rosie seemed more anxious now and she brought a hand to her lips for comfort.

'Don't worry. Could I just ask you a few questions? I'll buy us a coffee. I'm a private investigator,' Jo explained. It wasn't clear whether this reassured Rosie or not. She added a few more pleas, promising it would only take a few minutes.

Rosie stared at her and then turned away from the

window to speak to someone in the office. 'Do you mind if I go on my break now? I've got to see someone.' The other woman agreed and Rosie turned back to Jo. 'All right, I'll see you in the café in a couple of minutes.'

Chapter Eleven

'Found someone!' Jo announced triumphantly to Macy when she rejoined him on a bench outside. 'There's a Rosie who works in the box office.'

'I thought you were looking for an actress? Or a dancer.'

Jo shrugged. 'Maybe she likes to glamorize her job a bit. Come on, I'm meeting her for coffee in a second.'

Macy and Jo found a table in the narrow café, which looked out on the river. It was warm, crowded and noisy. Jo bought three coffees with biscuits and they sat in silence, with Jo giving every woman who came in a second look. Rosie eventually arrived, wearing just a vest and jeans, and looking self-conscious, she weaved between the tables towards them.

'What's all this about?' she asked, looking down at them both doubtfully.

Jo waved a hand towards the empty seat. 'Come on, I only want to ask you a couple of things. This is David Macy. He's my boss.'

'Just ignore me. I thought I was off duty today.' Macy gave Rosie a quick confidential smile and she sat down.

'What, are you really private investigators?' Rosie looked from Jo to Macy obviously curious. 'You must be following some poor woman's husband, are you? Why do you want to see me? Is it someone I know?'

'Well, it's a bit confidential. Have you worked here long?' Macy asked, interrupting Jo's intended explanation.

'Three months. It's just one of my part-time summer jobs,' Rosie said.

'What do you do the rest of the time?' Macy asked, giving her all his attention. Jo was irritated and amused by his obvious flirting. She would have gone about the interview in a more straightforward way but, observing the success Macy was having, she sat quiet.

'You'll never guess,' Rosie said, taking a preliminary sip at the froth on her coffee. 'Go on.'

'A librarian,' Macy suggested seriously.

Rosie looked at Jo. 'Is he joking or what?'

'Just ignore him,' Jo advised.

'Actually I'm a dancer,' Rosie announced, 'a professional. But I have to do another job to maintain my standard of living. You know how it is.' She sipped more coffee and smiled at Macy. 'So what do you want, then? Who's this naughty husband you're following? Go on, you can tell me.'

'Sean Fitzpatrick,' Jo answered directly.

Rosie's mascara-covered lashes flickered over her coffee cup. She replaced the cup on its saucer and turned her face to look at Jo. 'Who?' she said deliberately. 'I've never heard of him.'

Jo had never been more convinced someone was lying. 'You see, we are being paid to find out why he died,' she said matter of factly, still watching Rosie's bland expression.

'Oh, really.' Rosie's eyes wandered around the café and she looked noticeably less assured. 'Funny job you do,' she remarked, bringing her gaze back to Macy.

'Pays the bills.' Macy shrugged. 'You didn't know this Sean, then?'

'No. Should I? I meet lots of people. Have you got a picture?'

Jo produced one and Rosie studied it carefully and then shook her head. 'So he's dead, is he? How did he die?'

'He was hit over the head and left in a wood near

Draycote Water. Near the Castaway,' Jo explained, and then took a new tack. 'It's a pub – not far away – between Leamington and Coventry. Do you know it?'

'Vaguely. I might have been there once or twice. I think they have barbecues sometimes.'

'Do you remember going last month? About two weeks ago?' Jo asked.

Rosie laughed, a peal of real amusement that made people look round. 'My God,' she said, 'I have trouble remembering the pub I went to last night, let alone two weeks ago.'

'Someone saw you there with this man on June the eighteenth,' Jo said. 'It was a Friday.'

Rosie looked concerned. 'Did they? This is a bit serious, isn't it? If they go around telling the police that, I'll be at the bloody police station answering questions before you know it. Who's making these things up?'

'I can't say,' Jo answered. 'We haven't told the police anything. We're only interested because we're trying to find out what happened to Sean that night. Were you there?'

Rosie shook her head. 'No. I know where I was on the eighteenth because Fridays are my dance practice nights. You can ask my partner Dean Hampton if you like. He's been my partner for the last three years and we practise twice a week at the moment for the Midlands Championships.'

'Oh, that sort of dancing,' Macy interrupted again. 'Ballroom dancing, isn't it? You must be quite good to get into the Midlands Cup.' Rosie looked at him in surprise, which Jo felt probably mirrored her own expression.

'We've been finalists the last two years but never won. Anyway' – she tossed her pony tail over her shoulder and stood up – 'I'll have to go back now. It's the end of my break. Thanks for the coffee and the warning. I'll try not to bump into any policemen for a while. It looks like someone's got me mixed up with someone else.'

'By the way,' Macy asked as he got up to walk back with her, 'do you ever say you are an actress?'

'Actually I do act a bit,' Rosie said conspiratorially. 'Mainly I'm a dancer, though.'

'Do you work at Greenaways as well? The sports club in Leamington?' Jo butted in, determined not to let Macy take over completely.

'No. Look, I've got to get back now—'

'Just tell us your number so we can get in touch. Please?' Jo added as the other girl paused outside the box office.

Rosie rattled off a telephone number, which had Jo scrabbling in her bag for a pen and paper. 'Hold on a minute' – she wrote quickly – 'just one more thing: what car do you drive?' She realized this might be her last chance to ask Rosie anything. This meeting had been a bit of a disappointment after all that searching for her.

The tall girl shook her head and said she couldn't afford a car. 'Ask Dean if you don't believe me. He works at Cassidy's, the bar in Coventry,' she said over her shoulder. She seemed unconcerned. 'He'll be able to tell you where I was that night.'

'That flirting was so blatant,' Jo complained to Macy as they left the theatre and started to walk back to the car.

'I thought she was rather blatant with me actually,' he said smugly. 'Anyway it worked, didn't it? What would you have done?'

'I would have tried to get her on my side. As it is, we didn't get much out of her. I'm sure she knew who Sean was. And she could have been the girl I saw in Greenaways but I'm not sure. Then why would she say she didn't work there? That seems a pointless sort of lie. It's so easy for us to check.'

Macy had to agree with her about that. They were passing a pub and he suggested a drink.

Jo smiled as another idea occurred to her. 'I wouldn't mind,' she said, 'but that place is full of posers. What about trying Cassidy's?'

Macy pointed out that if Rosie was at all concerned about her alibi she would have rung her friend Dean to warn him to back her up but by then Jo was already driving them in the direction of Coventry.

The bar was in a converted bank: one of those banks that was built in the days when banks tried to look safe and impressive instead of fashionable and friendly. It was vast inside and the few people sitting around over the newspapers or idly chatting were dwarfed by the great pillars and sweeping central staircase. Jo and Macy sat down roughly where she used to queue to pay off her charge card debts. That was when she could afford debts, Jo thought to herself ruefully.

'I never eat roast dinners on Sundays any more,' Macy was saying. 'The demise of the roast dinner could be due to the disintegration of family life. Have you ever thought of that? I mean, when I was growing up, only alcoholics went to bars on Sundays and even then they came home for their Sunday dinner.'

A waiter approached and they both had to concentrate on the menu because this man was in a hurry. Although the place was not crowded, he strode up, whipped a cloth over the table and stood over them with pen poised. He treated any signs of dithering with such silent contempt that Jo ended up ordering the deep-fried calamari rings against her better judgement.

'Is Dean here?' Jo asked before the stocky man could rush off. She was fairly confident he was not a dancer. He moved more like a rugby centre-forward.

'I'll get him,' the waiter said abruptly and headed back to the bar.

'Certainly can't complain about the slow service,' Macy remarked.

A tall, slight boy brought their beers. He looked

younger than Rosie: maybe just twenty, Jo thought. He placed the glasses down on dainty paper bar mats and regarded them through curtains of blond hair, which fell from a central parting. He obviously knew they had asked for him and was waiting to find out why.

'Are you Rosie Martell's dance partner?' Jo asked politely.

'Yes,' Dean answered. He was cautious but not startled by the question. Perhaps Rosie had called him to warn him?

'Ballroom dancing, isn't it?' Macy said. 'What type do you do? You know, Latin American or what?'

'Mainly modern in competitions,' Dean answered, looking at Macy suspiciously. 'Why? Have you seen us dance?'

'No, we've just been speaking to Rosie,' Jo explained. She felt a bit sorry for Dean, who was clearly unsure if Macy was making fun of him. And she didn't want Macy to hi-jack another interview. 'We wanted to know where she was on June the eighteenth.'

Dean ran a finger along some spilt beer on the table and avoided looking at Jo. 'If it was a Friday or a Tuesday in the last six weeks, she was with me. Why do you want to know that?'

'Someone said they saw her in the Castaway. Do you know it?' Dean shook his head and Jo went on, 'And the same night a man was killed near there. His name was Sean Fitzpatrick. Have you ever heard of him? Or has Rosie ever mentioned him?'

'Don't think so.' Dean was still wary. 'You're not the police though, are you? So why do you want to know?' He tapped the empty tray against his leg in a repetitive movement.

'We were asked to find Sean. His brother was concerned about him. Now it turns out he's dead, his brother's even more concerned,' Jo explained succinctly.

Dean was shaking his head. 'It's nothing to do with

me and Rosie. We see a lot of each other at the moment because we're practising really hard for the Championships. It's very important. I'm sure Rosie wouldn't get involved with anything that might get in the way.' He broke off as if anxious he might have said too much.

Jo felt even sorrier for him but what he said was useful. What if these championships did mean a lot to Rosie and Sean had somehow got in the way? Was that ridiculously far-fetched? 'How long do you practise?' she asked.

'Three hours. Seven till ten. At least,' he added. He glanced around, shaking back his blond curtains 'I've got to go now.'

'Where could we see you dance?' Macy asked as Dean turned away. 'I'm very interested in ballroom dancing.'

The boy hesitated. 'Really?' he said with a forced smile. 'In a month's time our club is doing an exhibition at the Leofric Hotel. You won't need tickets, just turn up. Formal dress, though, I'm afraid.' He threw a little departing glance at Macy's clothes and walked away with more confidence than he had arrived.

'I don't believe either of them,' Jo remarked to Macy over her beer. For some reason both Rosie and Dean made her feel uneasy.

Macy's look was quizzical. 'What can we do about it?'

Jo did not have an answer to this at present so she turned to another subject that was bothering her. 'By the way, have you ever heard of Kelly Greenaway? She's the woman who owns that club I went to last night.'

Macy frowned. 'There's something familiar about the name – I'll look it up when I get back to the office. Of course I could have done that before you went if you'd kept me informed. I'm always the last person to know anything that happens—'

Jo wasn't listening. She was admiring the fancy gold plasterwork on the ceiling and wondering if Dean and Rosie were covering for each other.

Chapter Twelve

Jo told herself it was ridiculous to be nervous about an interview for a job she didn't even want but she did suffer the odd qualm while she was waiting to be called into the interview at the bank. It brought back those months of desperate job-hunting, when she had been trying to convince potential employers that her experience of travelling halfway round the world made her an asset to them. It didn't help either that her face was still showing the results of Saturday night's scrap with Rupert, the Dobermann.

She was sipping the obligatory lukewarm coffee when Vaz came over to her and said. 'Nick is ready to see you now.' His manner seemed to be very cool today, Jo thought, as she was led past Sean Fitzpatrick's office. The door was open and she couldn't resist staring in. What would she find in there? she wondered. Would an inspection of his office reveal more about the elusive Sean? She saw Vaz frowning at her and smiled back at him blandly.

Nick Walmsley had wonderful eyelashes. It was not the first thing Jo noticed but it was the most memorable. He was short and slight and seemed at home in his sizeable office. His handshake and his welcome were warm and definite. 'Jo.' He smiled as if he had known her all his life. 'How are you?'

Jo sat down and fielded the usual questions intended to put her at her ease. She concentrated not so much on her answers as on Nick himself, whom she found interesting. His suit and tie were sober and his light brown hair was neat. His hands remained clasped loosely in front of him but she sensed a suppressed energy about him. He conducted the interview in an affable, informal style.

Jo went through her prepared answers and it was difficult to know whether Nick Walmsley was impressed or not. He remained friendly throughout. His pleasant, deep-set eyes were difficult to read. At the end he asked if she had any questions and Jo had a chance to find out more about his colleague Sean Fitzpatrick.

'If I got the job, would I be working for Mr Fitzpatrick?' she asked.

Nick's smile did not alter but he shook his head. 'Afraid not. He's not with the bank any more. Do you know him well?' There was a fraction of a hesitation over the question. Nick must be guessing she didn't know about Sean's death and deciding it wasn't worth explaining.

'No, but he recommended the job to me,' Jo said. 'I believe he liked working here and thought it would suit me too.'

Nick gave a short laugh, which Jo wished she understood. 'Did he say that? It doesn't sound like him.' He did not elaborate but glanced at his watch, shuffled his papers and politely brought the interview to a close. Jo noted the ubiquitous framed photograph of wife and kids on the side of his desk, though he wore no rings. Here was Mr National Commercial Bank 1993, surely, she thought. And yet there was something about him which did not quite fit the image.

'One thing's for sure. If you do start work for the bank, there's no shortage of work for you,' he said amiably as he led her out of the office. His secretary was at her desk outside. 'This is Carol, she'll show you out. With two members of staff absent, work is building up all the time, isn't it, Carol?'

'Certainly is,' Carol, who Jo had seen showing out

the previous candidate, agreed enthusiastically. 'It's been chaos here the last few weeks, what with the auditors coming and going. Thank goodness that's over but I don't know how we're going to do without Sean and Cass. They had Securities taped between them. And your letters are piling up, Nick. I don't know when I'm going to get round to them.'

'Don't worry,' Nick placated her. 'You know what I always say: it's all under control. 'He flashed a grin at Jo. 'I always say it. Sometimes people are silly enough to believe it. Thanks for coming in.' He shook hands again and went back into his office.

'You can't fool me, I've known you too long,' Carol was saying and when Nick had disappeared, repeated it for Jo's benefit. 'He fools everybody else though,' she confided, 'bosses' darling. Can't do a thing wrong. My only hope is they keep promoting me alongside him. They have so far.' Carol led Jo back through the office. She walked briskly ahead in her sensible loafers. She was well dressed but Jo considered her clothes too middle-aged, guessing that Carol was only about her own age.

'I expect you've heard the news about Sean Fitzpatrick?' Jo asked, trying to get as much out of the talkative Carol as possible.

'Oh yes, isn't it terrible? Did you know him? I know it's an awful thing to say but in a way I wasn't surprised. Shocked yes, but not really surprised. Do you know what I mean?' Carol pressed the lift button.

'I think so. Of course I only knew him slightly,' Jo said encouragingly.

'I've had to see the police about him actually. They've taken over an interview room on the seventh floor and they want to see everyone who had anything to do with Sean.'

'Really? What did they want to know?' Jo tried to sound like she was asking out of idle curiosity.

'Oh, endless things.' Carol folded her arms over her

floral print dress. 'How long have I known him, was he any good at this job and suchlike. I tried to be diplomatic.' She paused to chew her lipstick worriedly. 'But you never know what conclusions they're drawing. Do you know what I mean?'

'I can imagine,' Jo sympathized, 'it sounds a bit harrowing. They wanted to know everything about Sean, then?'

'Yes. They asked if I'd had any leave in the last couple of weeks – which I haven't because it's been too busy. And what did I do the last two weekends? I said not much, I was too knackered after working at this place all week. It's been dire lately, it really has. They said he'd last been seen alive on a Friday two weeks ago. Creepy, isn't it?'

'How could anyone remember what they were doing on any one day like that?' Jo put in. 'I'm sure I couldn't.'

'Ah, well, Fridays are easy, you see. Friday nights Nick and I always work late because we're doing the reports for Monday. So it's quite normal for us both to be here until seven or eight o'clock.'

'You too? That's devotion to duty.'

'Tell me about it. People think being a PA is just typing letters but there's more to it than that – if you have a boss that gives you opportunities, of course.' On this decided note, Carol leaned forward and pressed the lift button again. 'Half the time I'm doing Nick's work.'

Jo fervently hoped it was a slow lift. 'You must know Nick very well.'

'I've been working for him for five years. He has his quirks – they all do. But he's good for my career and I can't argue with that.'

'What about Sean? He doesn't seem to have been as popular?' Jo heard the lift arriving behind her but it didn't prevent Carol from giving her opinion.

'To me he never was right for the bank at all. He used to like a few drinkipoos and a bet on the gee-gees – and he always seemed to me to be just on the brink of trouble. I sound heartless, don't I? Still, it comes to us all in the end. Only not so unpleasantly I hope,' she chuckled. 'You know the way out, don't you?'

Jo was sorry to have to leave Carol. She was a fount of information. However she didn't have much choice but to get in the lift when it arrived. It was while she was travelling towards the ground floor that she began to wonder. Would anyone notice if she went back to have a look in Sean's office? The only people likely to recognize her were Carol, Nick and Vaz. She would have to hope Nick and Carol stayed near Nick's office, which she wouldn't have to pass. Vaz had been working so diligently, with his head down over his desk, that she would be unlucky if he happened to glance up and see her.

Jo took off her visitor's badge, which she thought made her look more conspicuous, and dropped it into her pocket. The only way to do this was brazenly, she decided, and pressed the lift button to go back up. She strolled confidently out of the lift and pushed through the swing doors. She walked past one of the other interviewees, who was sitting on the edge of the easy chair. Seeing an apparently neglected blue file on a nearby desk, Jo picked it up and stuck it prominently under her arm. She could see Sean's door still stood ajar. The office was nearer Vaz's desk than she had remembered but his chair was empty. She looked round and couldn't see him so she took her chance, walked swiftly across to Sean's door and slipped in.

She closed the door behind her and made for the desk. It was cleared apart from a leather blotter and a calendar. There were some scribbles on the tired old blotting paper: doodles of horses, endless spirals and telephone numbers and names, which meant nothing to her. She tried the left drawer. Locked. The right drawer. Also locked.

She turned to the cabinet behind the desk. It opened

but it only seemed to contain files and stationery. The files were also meaningless to her. Each was labelled with a customer's name and an account number. Inside were printed lists showing transactions, she assumed, and the occasional letter about the account. She glanced at two and put them back, feeling frustrated.

She looked around the room for inspiration. There were no family pictures in this office. Either Sean had possessed austere tastes or the police had removed anything personal. Probably the latter, Jo guessed. In a cupboard she found a series of Lever-Arch files containing records of accounts going back five years. There was a half-empty bottle of Scotch and a glass, a single coffee mug and an opened bag of sugar. Sean was clearly not one for office hospitality. She sighed and stood up. She glanced over at the computer, which was on a separate table by the window, but decided it was not even worth switching it on. It was bound to be set up so that you couldn't access any of the files without knowing a password.

Her watch told her she had only been in Sean's room three minutes. She was reluctant to give up without finding anything useful but looking around the bare room she couldn't see anywhere else to search. Then she lifted her head slightly and noticed a cardboard box on top of the cupboard behind the desk. It was pushed to the back so it was not clearly visible. She was risking her limbs by standing on a swivel chair and reaching on top of the cupboard when the door opened and a voice said with quiet horror: 'My God! What are you *doing*?'

Jo swung round perilously quickly and the chair beneath her nearly did an extra revolution. She clung to the top of the cupboard for safety and it shuddered so that for a horrible moment she thought the whole lot was going to come down on top of her. She steadied herself, trying to maintain some panache, while staring down at Vaz, who looked outraged and anxious.

'I'm trying to get this box down,' Jo said, for once deciding that honesty was the best policy.

'I thought you'd left,' Vaz said angrily. But at least he still kept his voice down. Jo thought such presence of mind was promising. With some difficulty she got one arm around the cardboard box and began a tricky descent.

Vaz did not come to help her out. 'Did you know Sean Fitzpatrick is dead?' He went on in calmer tones, 'You can't go messing about with his private things. You know the police are here, don't you?' He watched as Jo put the box on the desk and started to rummage around in it. 'Security will have you out of here in thirty seconds,' he said seriously but she sensed he was more puzzled than angry now.

'I'm a private investigator,' she explained, somewhat breathlessly. 'I'm looking into Sean's death. You do know he was murdered, don't you?' She pulled out some old copies of the *Financial Times* and peered at the dates: June 16, 17 and 18. They were folded open on the markets page and some share prices were circled in blue pen.

'I heard rumours,' Vaz said cautiously, 'I didn't know for sure. Look, you can't stay here—'

Jo sighed over the papers. 'I suppose everyone who works in a bank has got shares in something or other. It doesn't mean much that Sean has circled these companies, does it?'

'What companies are they?' Vaz came over to the desk and looked at the paper. Jo had to hide a smile. Somehow she had always felt he would be on her side. 'Cereals, oil, retailing,' he was muttering. 'No significance that I can see. Investing on the stock market was a bit of a hobby with Sean, I think. He probably moved his shares about most days.'

Jo was looking further into the box. She had found two bottles of pills. She scribbled down the names so she could find out later why Sean was taking medication.

There was also a squash racket and some smelly old trainers. 'What is all this stuff?' she said, mainly to herself.

'I told you. They're his personal things. The ones the police didn't take. I put them in a box. I'm going to offer them to his next of kin when I get round to it. I believe he has a brother—'

'Yes, that's who I'm working for. I can take this box to him if you like,' Jo said hopefully.

Vaz was not having this, however. 'No. I'm keeping it here for the time being. The police may come back for it. Look, you'll have to go,' he said determinedly. He glanced around desperately and then turned his worried face to Jo. 'I've got something for you that might help. But you must promise to go if I give it to you.'

Jo agreed readily and Vaz told her to wait a minute while he went back to his desk. 'It's quiet out there now,' he said when he came back in, 'most people are at lunch. It's a good time to get you out.' He handed her a piece of paper with a name, address and telephone number on it. 'Get in touch with Cass. She might be able to help you.'

'Why? Who is she?' Jo asked, allowing Vaz to lead her out. She waited while he leaned out of the door. He gave her a quick nod and she ventured out. Trying to look as businesslike as possible, they walked side by side towards the lifts.

'She's the girl whose job you've just been interviewed for,' Vaz answered grimly while they waited for the lift to arrive. 'Don't ask me too many questions. I want to stay out of it. Just go and see her.'

Unfortunately for Jo, there was someone else in the lift, so she couldn't question him further until they reached the ground floor. Vaz, apparently determined to see her safely off the premises, accompanied her to the door but wouldn't say any more. As she walked away from the bank she could almost feel the intensity of his relief.

Chapter Thirteen

Jo tried Cass's number at the first telephone box she came to. It was unobtainable. Not very promising, she thought. Could Vaz have been just fobbing her off? She had no idea why he should choose to help her but decided it was still worth putting some effort into finding Cass.

People hurrying past clutching little lidded cups and paper bags of food made her feel hungry and she went into the nearest sandwich bar. The queue virtually reached the door but it was moving fast and she tagged on the end. She studied the blackboard above the counter. This was another of those places where she felt under pressure to choose and if she wasn't careful she would end up with either something hideous like a crab meat and beetroot sandwich or something boring like cheese and pickle. She had only read about a quarter of the blackboard by the time the woman behind the counter looked in her direction. Staying cool under pressure from the restive queue behind her, Jo chose a baguette filled with Brie and grapes.

She ate it standing up, leaning against a minuscule table in an ambience which was about as relaxed as a station buffet where everyone was expecting their train to be announced. She studied her *A-Z* and decided she needed the Tube to King's Cross.

Once there she had to consult it again and, when she was sure where she was going, set off down a road that seemed to be full of small hotels. Jo already knew from

Cass's address that she did not live in the most salubrious area. She made a few turns and the hotels became seedier. Here the shop windows were covered with wire mesh and houses were either boarded up or had bits of car engines in the front garden. Jo walked past a pub, where a very loud television shouted from the dark bar. A group of men standing outside with glasses in their hands made the most of Jo's passing to alleviate their boredom.

When she turned left again, she stopped in the next shop doorway. This was the kind of area where she wanted to look like she knew where she was going. She memorized the next few directions and dropped the *A-Z* into her duffle bag. With only one mis-turn, she ended up in the right street and walked past a bookies, a newsagents and an off-licence, looking for Cass's house. Virtually everyone who passed her stared at her, which did not make her feel any more comfortable.

She soon found it: a tall town house with walls that had been painted white once, steps up to a porch tiled with marked and cracked quarry tiles. Beside the large, peeling front door was a cluster of doorbells, some with names stuck on with yellowing tape beside them. Jo scanned them for a C. Baxter but Cass's name wasn't there. Eventually she rang one of the unnamed bells and waited. After trying three more bells, she finally heard promising shuffling noises from inside.

A woman about a foot shorter than Jo opened the door. She was elderly and faded. It took Jo a little while to establish that a girl who could be Cass had just moved into the top flat.

'Been chucked out by some man, I expect,' the older woman remarked, opening the door wider so Jo could step into the damp-smelling hall. Jo looked around at the aged mustard carpet, the pay phone with a sign saying *Out of Order* perched on top and the inevitable mound of mail on a flimsy table below. She was just about to start up the stairs when the woman leaned towards her conspiratorially: 'What do you want her for?' she asked, greedy with interest.

'I've just come on behalf of a work colleague to see how she's getting on,' Jo said airily.

'This girl doesn't work. I've never seen her leave this house yet except to get cigarettes and food.'

And I bet she wouldn't get by without you noticing, Jo thought to herself. The woman watched her start to climb the stairs and then shuffled off to her ground-floor flat and Jo heard a blast from the radio as she opened the door. It was an old house, though, and the sound did not travel once the door was closed. Jo carried on up the steep stairs. At each landing was a bathroom and toilet. She happened to glance in the open door of one and wished she hadn't.

The flat at the top was Flat 8. There was no mention of a flat number on the piece of paper Vaz had given her and Jo was doubtful that she had found the right place. She tapped tentatively at the door. There was no answer. She knocked harder. Still no answer. But it didn't feel like an empty silence. She waited and knocked again. She was sure she heard some movement but still nobody answered.

'Is Cass Baxter there?' Jo called. Her voice sounded hollow on the empty landing. She waited and listened to nothing at all. 'Vaz gave me your address. He said you might be able to help me.' She paused again. There was no response. 'I'm trying to find out what happened to Sean Fitzpatrick. You knew him, didn't you?'

Jo left a long gap before going on. 'In fact I was interviewed for your job this morning—'

'You can stick the job up your arse,' came a belligerent voice from surprisingly close to the door.

'I don't want the job,' Jo retorted irritably. 'I only went there in the first place to find out about Sean. Open the door, I want to ask a couple of questions about him.'

'Why do you want to know?' came the same aggressive female voice.

'I'll tell you when you open the door,' she answered doggedly.

'Piss off.'

She was almost inclined to take this advice. Her first impression of Cass Baxter didn't encourage her to get better acquainted. She moved away from the door and thought about one more question.

'Why did you leave the bank?' she tried.

'Why do you want to know?' the truculent voice demanded.

'I'm not explaining it through a bloody door,' Jo called back, annoyed. 'If you want to know why I'm here, open up.'

'You're not the police, are you?'

'No. I don't think they would hang around while you decided whether or not you were going to let them in.'

Whether this logic or persistence won, Jo never bothered to wonder, but Cass did finally open the door a grudging six inches. Jo could barely make out a slim figure with long hair and long clothes.

'Can I come in?' Jo asked patiently, wondering if she had to put on a repeat performance before progressing any further. But Cass only hesitated half a minute.

'All right. If you must,' she said reluctantly, holding the door wider. 'Only it's not exactly the Ideal Home Exhibition in here and I've got no tea.'

'It's all right, I don't like tea,' Jo said irrelevantly and walked past Cass into the bedsit. It was one small room with no division marking off the cooking area from the sleeping area. It had one long, narrow sash window and was untidy and not very clean. There were two cardboard boxes and a suitcase on the floor. Another lay open on the single bed with clothes tumbling out of it.

'Only just moved in?' Jo asked. She looked up at Cass, who still stood by the door. She was thin and scruffy, with unbrushed fair hair hanging either side of her face.

It had been highlighted with cheap reddish dye and made her face look even paler. Her dress was long and floral: the kind of thing she could possibly have worn at the bank but not with the ancient woolly cardigan which hung down to her knees and the men's grey socks on her feet.

'A week ago. Dump, isn't it?' Cass said looking round. She reached for her cigarette, which was lying on a saucer. She inhaled while risking a sidelong look at Jo through the parted hair.

'I've come to ask you some questions about Sean,' Jo said, 'but I know so little about him I don't really know where to start.' She looked out of the window to avoid staring either at Cass or the place. The view of a waste ground used as a car park was dispiriting. Cass said nothing. Jo sighed. 'All I know is: he worked for a bank, his brother's called Connor, who is a charmer I can't fathom out. I didn't like his mother—'

'Me neither,' Cass put in unexpectedly. 'Stuck up cow, talking down her nose and looking like she'd just stepped out of *Woman and Home*.'

Jo laughed. 'More like *Harpers and Queen*, if you ask me. Anyway, I just need to know anything you can tell me about Sean.'

Cass hadn't moved except to put her cigarette to her lips but she lifted her head to regard Jo more openly. Her face was white, undernourished and unhealthy looking, but she had attractive blue eyes and delicate features.

'I'm with you now,' Cass said, regarding Jo with some sympathy, 'you're another of his cast-offs, aren't you?' Cass leaned down to stub her cigarette out on the saucer. Jo didn't answer because an uncomfortable suspicion had drifted into her mind. Cass went on bitterly, 'He knows how to hump 'em and dump 'em, does Sean. I knew that before I got involved. Stupid cow that I am. He always was a bastard and he'll never change, I'll tell you that much.'

Now Jo was sure. Cass didn't know he was dead. Jo

didn't relish telling her but it had to be done. 'Actually,' Jo began, 'I'm not here because I was involved with him—'

'Well don't. That's my advice. Sean absolutely loves himself and no one else gets a look-in. Thinks he is the smartest, brightest bastard that ever lived. You know how he's always impressing you with how he got one over on somebody—' Cass came to a halt because she saw Jo's expression. 'Hang on. Have I got it all wrong as usual?' she asked.

'Well – I don't know how to tell you this. For some reason I thought you already knew. You see, Sean's dead.' Jo watched as Cass brought clenched hands to her face. Her eyes seemed to grow even larger. 'And what makes it worse,' she went on, 'he was murdered.'

'How? When?' Cass moved her hands to her mouth.

'He was hit over the head with something. The police haven't found the weapon as far as I know. It was in the middle of June.'

Cass swore. She stumbled towards the bed and sat on a pile of underwear. 'I suppose I ought to be pleased,' she muttered. 'I've wished him dead often enough. Christ only knows he deserves to be dead.'

'I'll get you something to drink,' Jo offered and made her way over to the kitchen area.

'I've told you, I've got no tea,' Cass said, her voice rising hysterically.

'There must be something else to drink,' Jo muttered to herself, as she opened empty dirty cupboards and an entirely bare fridge. There didn't seem to be any food at all.

'For Chrissake come and sit down!' Cass yelled. 'I told you there was nothing to drink.' She began to cry, still trying to take drags on her cigarette in between sobs and talking incoherently about Sean. Jo went over to try to comfort her and in the process managed to knock over a half-empty bottle of beer beside the bed. By the time she had found a cloth to mop it up, Cass had recovered a bit.

'It's all right. You wouldn't notice against this carpet anyway,' Cass said as she watched Jo sponging the floor. It did seem that the beer had sunk in without trace on the lurid patterned carpet. Jo abandoned the job.

'I had a nice place, you know,' Cass went on, wiping her face on a convenient towel from the suitcase. 'A flat in Notting Hill. I just couldn't afford the mortgage once I'd left the bank. I finally dropped the keys in the door of the building society the other night.'

'Why did you leave the bank? Because of Sean?' Jo asked.

'Vaz didn't tell you that, then?' Cass looked up. Her face was blotched but her eyes were dry now. 'I gave him this address because he insisted I keep in touch. He's a nice bloke. He was the only one who really seemed to care when Sean got me the sack.'

'Sean got you sacked from the bank? What do you mean?' Jo asked, startled. Then, seeing Cass's streaky, grimy face, she added sympathetically, 'Look, tell me about you and Sean and why you left the bank over a cup of tea. Is there somewhere we can go?'

'There is a café not too far away that does good buttered toast.' Cass blew her nose on the towel. 'I suppose we could go there. It would get us out of this hole for a bit.'

Jo was equally keen to leave the depressing room. She waited while Cass washed her face and found some shoes. They went downstairs and left the house, watched, no doubt, by the woman who had let Jo in. Still smoking, Cass seemed more prepared to talk now but she wanted to know why Jo was interested in Sean. On the way to the café, Jo explained. The fact that she was a private investigator brought no reaction from Cass, who was still preoccupied with Sean's death.

'It's hard to believe that he is actually not here any

more. Even though I never saw him, at least I knew he was on the same planet...' Cass said distractedly, 'What is difficult to swallow is that he was daft enough to get himself murdered. Sean always believed he could outsmart anybody, but someone must have borne a grudge, mustn't they?'

The café Cass had chosen was basic but clean. Jo ordered tea and toast for Cass and coffee for herself. 'When did you have to leave the bank?'

Cass took a bite out of the toast. 'Six weeks ago. It makes things worse, being sacked, because without a decent reference I can't get another job.'

'Surely it's pretty difficult for one manager to get someone sacked?'

'He said I'd stolen a hundred and twenty pounds. He said he'd had the cash in his jacket pocket. His jacket was hanging on the back of the chair in his office. I was always in and out of that room so he knew I would be one of the suspects. He reported the money missing to Nick Walmsley in the morning—'

'I met Nick this morning. He interviewed me,' Jo put in.

Cass shook her head balefully. 'Thick as thieves, Sean and Nick are. Or were. I wouldn't be surprised if Nick didn't know that Sean had set me up. He didn't waste any time calling the bank police in.'

'The bank police?'

'I know, it sounds like something out of Romania, doesn't it? But the NCB has its own police to investigate crimes amongst the staff. Banks take money very seriously,' Cass added with a glimmer of humour.

Jo began to like Cass, instead of just feeling sorry for her. Cass poured herself a cup of tea and took a few sips before going on. 'To cut a long story short, the bank police found the cash in my make-up bag. End of one brilliant career.'

'And Sean put it there?' Jo asked, not sure whether to

believe this or not. 'Why would he do that?'

'Sean put it in there that morning before we went to work. I was staying over at his place, which I usually did. He probably waited until I went to put my coat on and slipped it into the inside pocket of my make-up bag. It was a risk because I might have seen it if I had touched up my make-up before the police found it there. But Sean liked risks. That would have added to the fun of it for him.'

'And he knew you took your make-up to work and where you kept it?'

'That's right. Maybe he even told the police to have a particularly careful look in my desk because I had money problems.' Cass gave a short laugh. 'That would be a joke, when he was always the one who was thousands in debt.'

'But why would he do it?'

Cass shrugged. 'To get rid of me,' she said simply. 'He was fed up with me. I was past my use-by date. I was getting too involved, wanting to see more of him, asking him where he got to when he wasn't with me. That sort of thing. I could tell he thought I was too clinging but I just couldn't help myself.' She shook her head and sniffled.

Jo shook her head and stared at Cass. 'I can't believe he would do something so drastic just to finish the relationship. Why not invite you down the pub and tell you he had found someone else or other tried and tested methods?'

'That was part of the problem, you see. My jealousy. I was sure he was seeing someone else and I really gave him a hard time about it. That's why he got fed up with me.' Cass looked at Jo hopelessly. 'And I was so childish about it. That was what really pissed him off. I used to go through his pockets looking for evidence of the other woman and I even stole his address book because I was sure I'd find her name and number in there. I should have accepted that was the way he was...' Cass's voice tailed off miserably.

'No, you shouldn't,' Jo put in forcefully, 'he sounds a...' She paused in the middle of her diatribe as something occurred to her. 'Hold on, did you say you stole his address book?'

'Yes. I know that was stupid. I don't know what I expected to find. I couldn't tell which of the women in there was the one he was seeing. Or maybe he was screwing all of them. I did think of ringing them all up at one point, that's how bad I got.'

'I don't suppose you've still got the book?' Jo asked casually. Inwardly she was sure her sudden instinct was right and willed Cass to say yes.

'Yes.' Cass took a last sip of tea and hunted around in her capacious straw bag. Jo watched, riveted. After a moment Cass pulled out a slim black book with gold-edged pages. 'This is it.'

Jo took it, saying nothing. She was sure that this was the real reason Cass had been sacked before she even looked in it. There was nothing in the names and addresses to confirm her suspicion. It was just a list of people, most of whom lived in London, whose names she didn't recognize.

'Do you know any of these people?' she asked, continuing to turn the pages. Cass shook her head and Jo sighed. The book wasn't indexed and the addresses were not in any obvious order. It was less than half full and Jo flicked through empty pages, frowning. Then, near the back, she found a list of numbers. She showed them to Cass. 'What are these?'

Cass stopped rubbing her nose with her palm and looked at the book. 'Account numbers,' she said absently.

'I thought so. Whose account numbers? They couldn't all have been Sean's, could they?' There were about fifteen numbers in a neat line down the page.

'Doubt it.'

Jo stood up. 'Come on. You're still on speaking terms with Vaz, aren't you?'

'Yes, I rang him just the other day to give him my new address. Why?' Cass followed Jo out of the café as she made for the phone box she could see three blocks away. When they got there she called the bank and asked for Vaz. Cass, squashed in beside her, looked over her shoulder at the account numbers in Sean's address book.

'Vaz. It's Jo. I met Cass and I think we might be able to help her at least get a decent reference from the bank. Will you help?'

'What are you on about?' Vaz asked calmly, pouring cold water on Jo's excitement. 'I can't write Cass a reference.'

'No. I just want you to check out some account numbers for me. It may prove Cass was right about Sean getting her the sack. Can you do that reasonably easily?'

'Well—' Vaz hesitated. 'What are these accounts? What do you want to know?'

This temporarily threw Jo as she had not thought it out this far. 'Just who the account belongs to, how much money is in it, that sort of thing,' she said vaguely. Eventually, after Cass had added her pleas, Vaz agreed to run the numbers through the computer but said it would have to wait until most people had left the office. Jo said she would ring him back tomorrow morning.

'Of course, nothing may come of it,' Jo said belatedly to Cass when they left the phone box, not wanting to raise her hopes. 'Could I keep the address book, by the way?'

Cass looked doubtful. 'Well, no, not really. I know I won't get my job back but if this little item will help me get even with NCB—' she patted the side of her bag with a vengeful smile – 'I'm going to hold on to it. After all, it's a lot more important to me than it is to you,' she added reasonably.

Jo had to give up reluctantly. Before she left, she had

to broach something else to Cass, which might complicate her life still further. 'Have you ever been to Coventry?' she asked.

'No. Why?'

'That's where Sean was killed,' Jo said, shooting her a sidelong glance.

'In Coventry?' She sounded surprised.

'Well, on the outskirts. In a little wood near a pub and a reservoir.'

'The pub doesn't surprise me, but the rest of it does.' Cass frowned. 'What was he doing there?'

Jo sighed. Clearly Cass was not going to throw any light on this perennial question. But Jo felt she had to warn her that if the police ever heard her story she would be a major suspect. Jo tried to explain this but she seemed unconcerned. She said she didn't think the police would link her with Sean. 'Who knows except you?' she pointed out. 'Some people at the bank knew about Sean and me but they will have forgotten who I was by now. No one but Vaz has my new address and I think I can trust him.'

'If the police do find you, the first thing they'll ask is what you were doing on June the eighteenth,' Jo said. 'Oh, and do you have a car?'

'Never owned a car. No idea what I was doing on that day,' Cass answered promptly. She gave it a bit more thought due to Jo's prompting but still could not remember much. 'I was here in London looking for a job, I think.'

'Well, if you remember the names of anyone you met that day, you might find they come in handy,' Jo advised. And that was how they left it. Jo would not have been so relaxed in Cass's position. She didn't think the police would swallow Cass's story as readily as she had. It wasn't until she was on the Tube, going towards Putney, that her suspicious nature reasserted itself and she began to wonder why she had.

Chapter Fourteen

Jo could have spent another useful half-hour with Cass, trying to find out more about Sean, but Connor had called her that morning and invited her to dinner with his family.

'You said you wanted me to get you an interview with my mother,' Connor had reminded her, 'I've done better than that. You can meet the whole crew tonight and I've told them they have to answer your questions. The only drawback is, you have to accompany me.'

Truth to tell, that wasn't much of a drawback, Jo thought to herself guiltily. She knew that succumbing to Connor's charm was a mistake from a professional point of view and from a personal one. She still didn't trust him but of course she agreed to go, knowing it was a golden opportunity.

'Quite right,' Macy said when she called him to tell him her plans for a change, 'you don't pass up chances like that. You go and see if you can find any skeletons lurking in the family cupboards.'

Macy would probably encourage her to sleep with Connor if he thought it would further the case, Jo thought cynically as she turned into the road where Connor lived. She had timed it about right. He was just getting out of his car as she came up to his house. The way he glanced up and down the street as he locked his car made him look almost furtive but then he saw her and his expression changed.

'How are the mean streets, Jo? And how is the weary

gumshoe?' He seemed genuinely pleased to see her.

She grinned back at him. 'Well, it's the mean streets of Richmond upon Thames for me this evening, anyway.'

'I can promise you a decent dinner, if nothing else.' Connor held the front door open for her and followed her in, dumping his car keys, briefcase and jacket at strategic points on his way to the kitchen. 'Come in and have a drink to set you up for it.'

'How has your family taken Sean's death? Wouldn't it be better if I didn't butt in? I'm sure your mother doesn't want me around.'

'Probably not,' Connor agreed, gathering up the breakfast dishes and depositing them in the sink. 'But here you are now. They've not taken it too badly, I suppose. Or maybe it just hasn't sunk in yet.' He looked up from under a stray lock of hair and Jo noticed he seemed pale and stressed. 'It's getting to me though,' he admitted, 'especially after the gruelling hours the police put me through.'

Jo watched, leaning on the kitchen worktop while he rinsed and dried two glasses. 'I met someone interesting this afternoon,' she remarked, 'one of Sean's girlfriends. Do you know her? Her name is Cass.'

'Yes, she was an old girlfriend,' he answered easily. 'Old by Sean's standards, anyway. They must have been together at least three months.'

'Why didn't you mention her before? She said she used to stay here overnight so you must have met her.'

'Well, yes—' Connor shrugged and reached for a bottle of Bacardi from a kitchen cupboard. 'But they split up some time ago. She had left the bank so it was well and truly over.'

'But didn't you think of contacting her when Sean went missing?'

'No. Well, yes, I did think of it,' Connor answered thoughtfully, 'but I ruled it out. Unless I was going to hunt out all Sean's old girlfriends, there didn't seem much point.'

As always with Connor, Jo didn't know whether to believe him or not. He passed her a glass of Bacardi with tonic and lots of ice.

'Coke?' he offered and for half a second Jo thought he was going to top up her drink. Then she looked up and saw him delicately lining the powder up on a place mat. He took a drink straw out of a drawer and put it to his nose, pressed one nostril with long fingers and inhaled. 'I need this to be able to face my mother's dinner parties,' he told her brightly.

Jo's doubts about Connor redoubled. She shook her head. 'Not for me. I'll settle for some booze and my best efforts with make-up. Is there anywhere I can get changed?'

Connor, not yet noticeably affected by either the drink or the cocaine, was obliging as ever. He showed her to Sean's bedroom. It looked tidier and Jo remarked on this.

'Oh yes. That was the police. They were here all day Saturday. Took a load of stuff away with them and said they would come back for more. Of course they don't explain what they're doing. I'm off to shower now, just come down when you're ready.'

Before getting changed, Jo had another look round the bedroom. Sifting through the papers now in piles on his desk, she came across the bank statement which showed the cash withdrawal from the Coventry bank on June 18th. She looked back a month to around the time Cass had been sacked and saw a cash withdrawal for £120, the amount which she said had been planted in her make-up bag. It certainly supported Cass's story and Jo slipped it into the pocket of her holdall.

She took out the dark blue vest dress she had brought with her and examined it for creases. It had travelled well but somehow she felt that no matter how hard she tried to look her best she was not going to feel at her ease.

This instinct turned out to be true. If she had remembered Mrs Fitzpatrick as being elegant, she had underestimated her. The woman was a beauty. Her pale hair was piled on her head; her earrings glinted discreetly and she looked sinuously thin in a pearl grey silky suit which made Jo feel brash in comparison. She looked pale but greeted Jo with a gracious smile. She gave Connor a little light hug but held on a moment longer than he did.

'I'm sorry,' she said weakly, her head turned away, 'I'd never noticed before how much alike you and Sean were—'

Connor looked desperate but tried to be comforting. 'Come on, don't cry now, and we can't leave Jo on the doorstep—'

'I'm sorry about Sean,' Jo said awkwardly.

Fiona Fitzpatrick accepted Connor's handkerchief and dabbed at her eyes. She turned to Jo. 'Oh yes, we've met, haven't we? Hello,' she said distantly, extending delicate long fingers, 'I do hope you're not going to ask us hundreds of tedious questions about poor Sean. I don't think I'm up to it.'

'I'll try not to,' Jo murmured, reflecting that you needed all the sensitivity of a rhinoceros to be a good PI. She was obviously developing this quality because she followed dutifully into the house.

'It's such a warm evening, we're on the lawn at present,' Fiona said, seemingly recovered. 'I'd love to dine outdoors but Connor's father thinks it's uncomfortable so we'll eat in the conservatory as a compromise.'

It was hard to imagine Fiona Fitzpatrick as anyone's mother but Jo noticed that she took a maternal interest in Connor. While her polite chatter was directed at Jo, her eyes looked him over and she swept him off to help with the drinks as soon as she had introduced Jo to the other guests: 'Just the family,' as she put it.

In the cab on the way over, Connor had described them all so Jo could easily identify them before she was introduced. 'The miserable old bugger who moans about everything from the M25 to the price of fresh salmon is my father. My elder brother Kieran tries to be exactly like him and his wife Gina will be tottering around on her high heels making comments about the weather.'

In fact Connor's father, Gerrard, was in the middle of a diatribe about the deficiencies of the education system but he broke off to shake hands with Jo. 'How do you come to know Connor? Through business, is it?' He could, unlike his wife, be described as middle-aged. He was dark and thick-set, with little resemblance to Connor apart from something about the set of the shoulders and Connor's enigmatic expression.

'Yes, business,' Jo said pleasantly. 'I'm a private investigator. Connor is employing my firm.'

'Oh yes, you're that one, are you? Connor said something about you.' Gerrard Fitzpatrick regarded her for a moment and then looked out over the lawn. 'Can't the police be relied upon for that sort of work? Or is Connor just being unconventional as usual?'

'He doesn't strike me as particularly unconventional,' Jo remarked but Gerrard began speaking over her reply.

'Remarkable how well Connor is doing, you know. Only thirty and he's already a partner. We're very pleased with him.'

Jo couldn't work out whether this was meant as information for her benefit or to warn her that Connor was out of her league. 'He and Sean were close,' Gerrard went on, frowning at her. 'It's been a great shock to us all.' Before she could respond, Connor and his mother came back with the drinks.

'Gerrard, have you been dominating our guest? Haven't you let her talk to the others yet? Come with me, Jo.' Fiona placed a glass of pale cold sherry in Jo's hand and introduced her to the couple on the terrace who Jo had noticed were sitting in silence.

'Nice to meet you,' Kieran said politely. With his dull sports jacket and bored eyes, Jo decided he was distinctly less charming than Connor. His wife, who looked out of place in white dungarees and high heels, said a quick hello and then sat back, sipping a long drink.

'Jo is my private investigator,' Connor said, pulling up heavy wrought-iron seats for himself and Jo.

'Are you making so much money you need a minder now?' Kieran responded lazily.

'I'm trying to find out some more information about your brother Sean,' Jo answered coolly. 'Can't you tell me anything about him?' When this brought no response, she added, 'For instance, do you know who might want to kill him?'

'He had friends in low places,' Kieran said casually, 'I've put his death down to the company he kept—'

'What sort of people?'

Kieran frowned at her. 'Well, I don't know them, for God's sake. I had very little to do with Sean and the family had pretty well washed their hands of him—'

'Except for Connor,' Jo put in, catching Connor's eye.

'Well, I've said I didn't know what he was up to half the time,' Connor said, sounding embarrassed. A little awkward silence fell. Jo took a sip of the excellent sherry and asked with slight sarcasm if they could think of anything else helpful.

As the two men said nothing, Gina leaned towards Jo earnestly. 'Well, he was very good with figures,' she said knowledgeably. Jo wondered how to respond to this. Gina smiled at her ingenuously from under a fringe of red hair. 'What are you wearing to the funeral? Do you think it's over the top to wear a veil? I'm not a blood relative, you see.'

'I would think it would be all right,' Jo said vaguely, aware that the two men had started talking to their father. Remarks about golf shots reached her ears while Gina told her confidingly about her problems over choosing a suitable outfit.

'I don't look very good in black, do you?' Gina was saying seriously when they were called in to dinner.

'No, it always makes me look washed out,' Jo heard herself say as she went into the conservatory at Gina's side. She almost clutched her head in despair. This was not going to get her anywhere.

The food was light and varied but the conversation didn't match. Gerrard and Kieran were both doctors and most of their conversation turned on hospital politics. Fiona's comments were limited to accommodating remarks or occasionally, like a good hostess, to encouraging the quieter ones to join in.

Jo had been surprised by Fiona's emotional scene on the doorstep but it seemed positively unreal that throughout the meal Sean's name was not mentioned once. She couldn't let them get away this lightly. She didn't bother being subtle, because if she waited for an opportunity, one might not arise. During a lull in the conversation, she asked politely, 'Does anyone have any idea why Sean would have come to Coventry?'

Fiona Fitzpatrick was the first to recover. 'I've really no idea. Maybe you are best placed to say, Jo? What does Coventry have to recommend it?'

'Well, I don't think he went to visit the cathedral.' Jo looked round at the family, who all looked uneasy. 'I'm sorry to press this. But I have to try to find out what I can.'

'We've no connections with the place,' Gerrard responded tetchily, 'as I told the police countless times. Sean was his own man—'

'Oh, yes, we had the West Midlands Police Force tramping all over the carpets the whole weekend,' Fiona said, her gaze sweeping round the table, 'and I found something out about policemen. They all take three sugars in their tea. To a man. Isn't that interesting?'

There was a polite laugh. Jo sighed and helped herself to more salad. She knew Sean had been the middle son of three and one thing that occurred to her, as she let the salmon mousse linger on her tongue, was that in this family circle of consultants and stockbrokers, a middle manager of a bank would not shine very bright.

After the meal, they moved to a comfortable room indoors and the whisky decanter was produced. Connor, accepting a second glass very quickly, became more loquacious and she heard him advising Gerrard about what car he should buy. While Jo was wondering about her chances of persuading him to call a taxi soon, Fiona came up to her, preceded slightly by her perfume.

'How are your investigations going?' she asked in the same reserved, civil tones Jo had been hearing all evening.

'I'm making slow progress.'

'I just wanted a little word.' Fiona lowered her voice. 'You know we care deeply about Sean.' Her dark eyes looked into Jo's and Jo noticed that her eye liner was still near perfect. She murmured something suitable in reply and Fiona went on, 'It's just that Connor's too young and idealistic to see it but we don't want a lot of fuss made. Of course we want to know what happened to Sean, but I've every faith in the police, so why don't you let Connor have a nil return?'

The conspiratorial note in her voice annoyed Jo. 'That wouldn't be very professional of me, would it?'

'Dear me, I hadn't realized private investigators thought of themselves as a profession.' Fiona gave a trill of laughter.

'I have to do the job I am paid for,' she said icily. Out of the corner of her eye she could see Fiona's husband bearing down on them.

'Are you getting tired, darling?' he asked his wife solicitously. 'We shouldn't be up too late, not with tomorrow on the horizon.' Jo didn't entirely understand this but she was more than ready to leave. Fiona was staring back at her coldly. Jo got up without speaking and went to find Connor.

He was pouring himself another whisky and when he

looked up at Jo, his eyes were distinctly unclear. She told him tersely that she was going home and would be in touch about the case. Connor insisted in his usual easy manner that she mustn't go without him. He put down his glass and went out to call a cab for both of them. Jo's anger had died down and left her with an intense feeling of boredom. She hesitated a moment and then followed Connor into the hall.

It seemed the little party was breaking up anyway. Kieran and Gina followed her out. Kieran was talking over his shoulder to his father. Gerrard Fitzpatrick apparently wanted to show his son some new security lights he had bought for the garage doors.

'Wait there. I won't be a minute,' Kieran said curtly to his wife before he went after his father.

Gina folded her arms across the bib of her dungarees and leant against the staircase. 'How boring,' she said darkly to Jo.

'It doesn't sound like you're missing anything exciting,' Jo agreed, looking round for Connor.

Gina gave an unexpected giggle. 'I know that,' she said. 'Exciting is not the word for anything that happens in this house.' She had a soft face: her features indistinct apart from her small mouth.

'How do you put up with this supercilious bunch of hypocrites?' Jo wondered aloud.

'You don't mean that about Connor, surely?' Gina grinned slyly. 'He's the spoilt baby of the family. He can do no wrong.'

'Not like Sean,' Jo commented, 'no one's got a good word to say about him.'

'He was the black sheep. Not clever like the others – or even nice-looking. I think he misbehaved just to draw attention to himself like kids do.'

'People keep saying things like that, but what did he actually do?'

Gina dropped her voice to a whisper. 'There was the

drugs and gambling and his marriage. His wife ended up hating him. I never blamed her for leaving like she did—'

'Who was she? What happened to her?'

'Valerie? Left the country, I believe. He met her at the bank. She had nobody but him and she worshipped him—'

'Do you have to leave now, Jo?' Fiona's distinct voice cut across them. 'Connor tells me he's called a cab.'

'Yes. Thank you for the lovely meal and for bringing yourself to be so polite to me,' Jo answered sweetly. Gina took a step away from Jo, not wanting to be associated with such daring. Connor, who appeared from behind his mother, seemed unabashed. He regarded Jo with wide-eyed amusement.

Fiona regained her poise after only a moment – but Jo enjoyed that moment. The doorbell gave a muted ring and Connor cut through the edgy little group of women to answer it. 'Cab's here,' he announced, holding the door for Jo.

'You shoot from the hip, don't you?' he remarked affably to her as they walked down the drive. Jo was quite surprised when he got in the cab with her. She wouldn't have cared one way or the other but she saw him grinning at her and started to laugh.

The whole evening suddenly seemed hilariously funny. She recounted her conversation with Gina about what to wear at the funeral and they both roared hysterically. Recovering first, Jo called out to the taxi driver to take her to Connor's address, adding that she would go on to Euston Station.

'No,' Connor protested, 'you must stay with me tonight. I've got a very good sofabed. Or you can have my bed – with or without me in it.'

'No, I want to get home,' Jo said. But Connor went on persuading her, promising her the sofabed and complete privacy, and eventually she gave in. The amount Connor had imbibed, she didn't think he would be capable of anything remotely sexual and she believed him when he said he would not try.

'What was Sean's wife like? Why did they get divorced?' Jo demanded of Connor, who was slumped in one corner of the cab, still giving the occasional giggle. 'Could she have borne him a serious grudge?'

'Valerie?' Connor focused his eyes on her with obvious difficulty. 'Shouldn't think so. She was a bit of a drip. I told you he used to beat her about a bit, didn't I?'

'Not in so many words,' she said coolly. 'Is that why she left him?'

'I should think so.' Connor roused himself to look out of the cab window just as they turned into his street.

'And her name was definitely Valerie – not Rosie?' Jo suggested.

'Shit!' Connor said suddenly and dived down to the floor of the cab. 'Don't stop,' he said urgently to the driver, 'keep going.'

'What's wrong?' Jo asked, alarmed. 'Are you OK?'

The driver swore and demanded to know where he was supposed to go.

'Anywhere – just quickly. For Christ's sake, don't stop!' Connor shouted, still crouched on the floor of the cab. He tried to pull Jo down with him but she stared out of the window as the cab drove past the house. Two men were sitting on the garden wall looking around them. As the cab went past, one of them stood up to stare at it.

'Who are they?' Jo asked, turning her head to watch them as the cab passed.

'Where the bloody hell am I going?' the taxi driver bawled.

Connor got up gingerly. 'A hotel—' he muttered. Jo thought she had never seen anyone sober up so fast. His face was white and his eyes terrified.

'Whereabloodybouts?' the taxi driver demanded. Connor named a hotel in Bayswater. He licked his lips and held his throat as if desperately thirsty.

'What was all that about?' Jo asked, looking at him.

'I'll tell you when we get indoors,' Connor answered faintly. Jo desisted. She decided she had better let him get over the shock. Predictably, his first question at the hotel was to find out how he could get a drink. He ordered a bottle to be brought up to his room. Unquestioningly he booked two, one room for himself and one for Jo, but she followed him into his. She had no intention of staying there but she wanted an explanation before finding her own bed.

'Wait,' Connor said, when she started to ask questions. He slumped on the side of the bed. His hair hung over his bloodshot eyes and his tie knot lay limply on his chest. Jo waited. There was a knock at the door and the bottle of whisky arrived. Against her better judgement, she poured some into a tooth glass for him. Connor drank it and refilled it himself.

Jo sat down on a chair on the opposite side of the room. She was feeling a bit shocked herself. She had never seen a change come over anyone as suddenly as this. She knew it was the effect of the coke and drink as much as anything else but she still felt oddly disillusioned. He looked at her, saw her expression and took another drink.

'Who were those men?' Jo asked calmly.

'Sean's creditors. They're after me for money,' Connor said simply.

'Much money?'

'Thousands – more than I can lay my hands on right now but I am trying.'

'Why pay? Why not just tell the police?' Jo knew it couldn't be as simple as that. She sat and waited. Connor put down the glass and said nothing. 'Is this something to do with your supply of coke?' Jo asked tonelessly.

Connor nodded. 'Sean was the dealer. I just bought some off him and now and again gave a little bit out to friends—'

'For money.'

'God, yes – that stuff is too expensive to just give away.'

'So you dealt too.' On one level, Jo found it hard to believe she was having this conversation. She knew nothing much about drugs. She had only ever smoked a bit of dope in her life. Half an hour ago she had even contemplated sleeping with this man. She wanted to believe that she was not having this conversation.

'Just to friends,' Connor was saying, 'Sean got hold of the stuff. Trouble is, he died owing money to his supplier. Don't ask me how, I don't know. Or maybe they're even lying about him owing them but it doesn't matter much because they're coming after me for it. I'm going to get it. I just need a few more days.'

'Why didn't you tell me about all this before? They could have had something to do with Sean's death.'

'Wouldn't make sense if he owed them money.' Connor sighed. 'I guessed it might have to come out but I wanted to avoid it if I could.' He gave Jo a wry look. 'This kind of thing wouldn't go down well at work. Don't go broadcasting it.'

'Who are these people? The men who were sitting on your garden wall?'

Connor looked at her hopelessly. 'I honestly don't know. The guy who rings me never gives a name. I know Sean used to meet someone in a club to get his supplies—'

'Which club?'

It was a little while before Connor answered and then she had to strain to hear. 'I don't even know which club. I didn't want to get too involved—' He gave Jo an ironic smile.

'How often have these men been in touch with you? Have you seen them before?'

He refilled his glass, spilling some whisky on to his hand. 'Never. Never before. It's the funeral tomorrow, you know. Are you going to be there?' He tilted backwards as he spoke, sliding into a prone position while still holding his glass upright.

'More to the point, are you?' Jo sighed, watching his eyes close. It seemed she was not going to get much more information out of Connor tonight so she told him she was going to bed.

'I'm fine. Don't worry about me,' he called as she let the door close softly behind her. Lying on her bed in her hotel room and listening to the noise of the traffic outside, Jo wasn't sure whether she wanted to carry on with this case. Any sympathy for Sean Fitzpatrick or his brother had evaporated. After ten minutes, she got up, went to the bathroom and vomited up her dinner.

Chapter Fifteen

Jo was in the same uncharacteristically depressed state of mind when she woke up the next morning. Room service delivered a pot of coffee and a plate of croissants, which she hadn't ordered, to her bedside.

'Thanks but—' Jo said blearily, fumbling for her watch.

'Mr Fitzpatrick sent these and says he'll pop in to see you in half an hour,' the waiter told her. 'It's twenty past nine,' he added sympathetically.

Jo poured herself a coffee and got up slowly. Outside the traffic roared down the Bayswater Road and it was raining. 'Good day for a funeral,' she murmured to herself. After her second coffee she stood in the shower for a long time and then dressed quickly, aware that Connor would be knocking on the door any minute.

Her head ached badly but a vague sense of duty prompted her to ring Vaz at the bank. She dialled his number while sitting on the edge of the bed taking disconsolate bites of a croissant.

'Hello, I thought you'd call,' Vaz said warily when Jo was put through.

'Did you get anywhere with checking those account numbers?' Jo asked, coming straight to the point. She was not in the mood for pleasantries.

'Yes, nothing special about them. They were all closed accounts.'

'Oh. Who did they belong to? Sean?'

'No. Various people,' Vaz muttered, clearly aware of

listening ears in the office. 'Why are you asking me to do this?'

'I'm concerned about Cass. Look, I know you can't speak freely but did you recognize any of the people these accounts belonged to? Were they all different?'

'Yes, all different. No, none I knew,' Vaz said briefly. 'How is she, is she OK?'

'Cass? Not particularly.' Jo sighed. 'Oh well, thanks for trying—'

'One thing,' Vaz added belatedly, 'they had all been closed recently.'

'Recently? Before June the eighteenth, though?'

'That's right. All closed in the month prior to that date. I have to go now.'

'Can you keep looking for something? I'm sure Sean closed all those accounts because Cass found out they existed. She doesn't know any more but there must have been something funny going on. Thanks, Vaz.' Jo put her fingers on her forehead and found she could pinpoint the ache. It was unfair to feel so bad when she hadn't even drunk all that much, she thought. Then Connor knocked at the door and she felt worse. She pulled on her jacket and went to open it. To her surprise, he looked his usual neat self.

'Sleep well?' he asked, sounding slightly subdued.

'Not really,' Jo said curtly.

'Me neither.' He gave her a rueful smile. 'I have to go back to Putney. Sean's funeral is in Richmond, St Thomas's at twelve o'clock. I'll settle up for us here and maybe see you...?' The question trailed off. He gave her a quick look and added, 'Or maybe not.'

'Either Macy or I will be in touch,' Jo said dutifully, remembering that this man was paying her wages.

'OK,' he acquiesced. 'Listen, I'm sorry about last night. I'm not going to make excuses but—'

Jo cut him short, saying she had to catch a train to Coventry. They walked down the corridor together,

Connor chatting genially as usual and Jo beginning to feel slightly more kindly towards him so that they managed to part on reasonable terms. She was glad to be left on her own again, though, to set off for Euston and home.

At the station she found that all trains bound for the Midlands were suffering delays due to vandalism on the track. She groaned aloud. For a while she couldn't think of anything else to do except stand around with all the other people, craning her neck to re-read the notice. Then it occurred to her that she should call Macy. He had probably been expecting her to let him know how she had got on at the bank yesterday. She joined a long queue by the phones and after a mindless wait found herself listening to Celia's indomitably cheerful tones.

'Thank goodness you've phoned, Jo. We've been wondering where you were. Mr Macy was ringing your flat last night and he even called round this morning in case your phone was out of order.'

'I suppose he expected me to report back.' Another thing that had gone wrong, Jo thought glumly.

'Well, yes, and I think he was a bit worried about you. Are you all right?'

'Mm, sort of – I suppose I ought to tell him the latest developments. You'd better put me through.'

'Oh, he's not here now. He's gone to Sean Fitzpatrick's funeral. He asked if you could meet him there if you called. Do you know where it is?'

Jo admitted, somewhat reluctantly, that she did. She didn't want to go anywhere but home. She certainly didn't want to go to a funeral. On the other hand, the journey home by train was obviously going to be slow. She found out from Celia that Macy had brought his car so she would be able to get a lift back to Coventry. She need not encounter any of the Fitzpatricks, she reasoned, and in any case she would probably be too late for the funeral. She hoped Macy would still be around. She told Celia she would meet him there.

Jo's day seemed to be improving. The rain had stopped before she reached Richmond. Then, as she walked up the hill, she saw Macy leaning against the churchyard wall. His shoulders were hunched, the collar of his dark jacket was turned up and despite his suit and tie he managed to look thoroughly out of place and suspicious.

'You'll give private investigators a bad name,' Jo advised as she came up to him.

'Oh, you've turned up at last, have you? You've missed the funeral. They've all packed off to the wake about five minutes ago.'

'Can't say I'm sorry.'

'Come on, let's go for a drink. You look terrible,' Macy said, looking at her face and frowning. He turned to walk beside her.

'You haven't got a Paracetamol, have you?' Jo asked, guessing it was the kind of thing Macy would have about his person. She was right. He led the way to a dark little pub on Richmond Hill, which was almost entirely empty at that time of day. He bought her a chilled bottle of mineral water and handed her two painkillers. Jo, absurdly, felt tears come into her eyes at this little kindness. God, I must be in a worse state than I thought, she said to herself and swallowed the tablets swiftly.

'So where did you get to last night?' Macy asked casually, looking around him.

'A hotel in Bayswater Road with Connor Fitzpatrick,' Jo said honestly and saw with some gratification that Macy's gaze became unusually focused. She told him about yesterday's events without going into details. He didn't ask many questions and kept glancing at the door when anyone came in. 'Are you expecting someone?' Jo interrupted herself to ask.

'Yes. Nick Walmsley, Sean's boss. I spoke to him after the funeral. He said he would just show his face at the Fitzpatricks' house and then would come down here for a drink.'

'Why do you want to speak to him?'

'I don't particularly. He was the only person there who didn't totally ignore me,' Macy admitted.

'That figures,' Jo laughed. 'He'll be surprised to see me. He was interviewing me for a job yesterday.' She did not have time to finish her report to Macy before Nick's smart-suited figure appeared at their table.

'Hi – dreadful occasions, aren't they, funerals? Can I get . . .' He paused as his eyes met Jo's. 'Didn't I see you yesterday?' As realization dawned, a palpably insincere smile began on his face. 'So you weren't a real candidate, then? Well, that's a good one. I suppose you have to be up to all sorts of tricks in your line of work. It's fortunate I didn't give you the job,' he added maliciously.

'It's all right, I wouldn't have accepted,' she returned.

Nick laughed uneasily. 'Let me get you both a drink anyway.'

'So Connor and Sean were into drugs and Connor has to find the money to pay off Sean's suppliers,' Jo said, finishing her story rapidly while Nick was at the bar. 'And I think Sean was involved in some sort of scam at the bank too.'

Macy looked exasperatingly vague but Jo guessed he had taken it all in. He smiled affably at Nick when he came back with the drinks. 'It's good of you to come. I need to find out as much as I can about Sean.'

'You don't want to trouble the family at a time like this,' Nick agreed, taking a seat, 'I'm quite happy to help if it takes some of the pressure off them. I've known Sean years so I can probably tell you anything you want to know.' He smiled at Macy over his pint. He hardly seemed to notice Jo, who was pouring out her second glass of water. She found it harder to trust his open-eyed expression since her conversation with Cass.

'You've known him years, you say?' Macy prompted, sipping his own drink.

'We were at university together in Manchester. We

were friends then and stayed in touch afterwards. I was working at the bank when Sean was looking for a job. His computer business failed so I suggested the bank and he got the job. I don't think he realized he would end up working for me, though.' He chuckled. 'That must have been a bit hard for him to take – as he was always supposed to be the brilliant one. That's often how it goes, though, isn't it? These bright sparks burn themselves out.' He hesitated, perhaps realizing that what he had said was too apt.

'You were close friends, then?' Macy asked before Nick could recover.

'Yes – as far as work allowed of course. Unlike Sean, I've got my career and a wife to think about so I couldn't always be at his beck and call, out on the town every night – you know the sort of thing.'

'I suppose you had to see the police and they took a statement,' Macy said lazily, his eyes wandering around the bar.

'Not just from me but from virtually everyone at work. And they even went to see my wife too, which I thought was a bit of a cheek.'

'Mm. So what did you say? In your statement, I mean?' Macy asked, sipping his drink.

'All they were really interested in was where I was the night Sean died.' Nick sat back in his chair and massaged his right shoulder absently, 'I was working late – not alone, fortunately for me.'

'Oh yes, with Carol, your secretary?' Jo chipped in.

'That's right.'

'She told me.' Jo thought this conversation was getting too cosy so she decided to take a hand. 'I also met Cass Baxter yesterday,' she put in brightly.

'Oh dear.' Nick sighed complacently. 'You do know she's got a chip on her shoulder, don't you?' He shot Macy a conspiratorial glance as if to recruit his sympathy. Macy, who was in saintly mode today, did not give him any encouragement, Jo noticed.

'Cass reckons Sean got her the sack and you helped,' she said. She had decided on a direct accusation so she could watch Nick's reaction.

He heaved another sigh. 'I know, I know. She's been to me with this story. But as I said to her, if she's got that good a case, she should take us to an industrial tribunal. She didn't seem too keen on that for some reason.' This was said with another smug glance in Macy's direction.

Macy buried his face in his pint glass. He left it to Jo to continue this line of questioning, although he must have wondered what she was on about as she had not had time to explain about Cass.

'She might have a better case than you think,' she said. Having decided to take the bull by the horns, there was no point in holding back now. 'You know about Sean's address book? It has some very interesting numbers in it...' Jo let this sentence tail off and watched him.

Nick was shaking his head sorrowfully. 'Ms Baxter has really led you up the garden path, hasn't she? Why should I be interested in a list of Sean's old girlfriends? I'm happily married.' He gave another little chuckle. But Jo noticed he was drinking faster. Most people slowed down towards the end of a pint but he had speeded up.

'So as far as you know, Sean wasn't up to anything dubious at the office?' Jo asked.

'No. We had the auditors in only a couple of months ago – they went away perfectly happy, so you don't just have to take my word for it.'

'And you would know?' Macy put in unexpectedly. 'I mean, if he was up to something, you would know – as his boss.'

'Of course. I can save you some time here,' Nick said pleasantly. 'You are going down a blind alley with this one. Sean may not have been totally respectable in some ways, but as far as the bank is concerned, he is as clean as a whistle.' Nick downed the last of his drink and set his glass down carefully. 'Speaking of the bank, I must be getting back to it. I hope I've been some help.' He got to his feet, his movements lithe and comfortable.

Jo and Macy thanked him and Nick made some remark about being glad the funeral was over. He left, walking briskly and looking as if he had already forgotten them before he reached the pub door. Macy looked at Jo and for once she knew exactly what he was thinking. 'Nick is involved, isn't he?'

'In shit up to his ears,' Macy said sweetly. 'And the clever thing to do next is to check his alibi.'

Chapter Sixteen

'I've already spoken to his secretary, Carol. She says she was with him until quarter past eight that Friday night so he probably couldn't have got to Coventry in time,' Jo said, thinking it over as she spoke.

'That's assuming the time of Sean's death ties in with the broken down Chevette in the lay-by and the blonde girl and so on but what if that is totally spurious?' Macy leaned across the table to talk. He had suddenly taken on one of his rare animated moods and Jo wondered if the moon had just changed signs. 'Say he died later,' Macy went on, 'then Nick could have got there.'

'How would Nick know where he was?'

'A minor point.' Macy dismissed it with a sweeping gesture which almost knocked over the mineral water bottle. 'The post-mortem was yesterday afternoon so the police should have a better idea of the time of death by now. And we want to know where Nick went after he left the office. I'll call Debbie. Won't be a minute.'

When Macy came back from his phone call to Sergeant Beatty, he was his usual gloomy self. 'They've put the time of death at between nine and ten p.m. Nick left the office at eight o'clock so it looks like he's in the clear.'

'I'm not convinced. Any other news?'

'Debbie says they've unearthed a few more witnesses who saw Sean on Friday the eighteenth. The last sighting was in the Castaway at about half-past eight. And they've found his car. It was in one of the car parks at Heathrow

Airport. No unusual prints but they're doing a thorough search now.'

'Did you find out where Nick went after work on Friday?'

'Yes. All very cosy and domesticated. He went home to his wife in St Albans. Mrs Walmsley supports his story but Debbie has some doubts about her. Do you fancy a visit to wifey?'

'You mean your pal Debbie gave you the address?'

'We did a swap. I told her what Alan's found out about the Chevette.'

'Well, that's more than I know,' Jo said peevishly.

'I forgot to say: Alan found a garage mechanic who remembers selling it only a few weeks ago to a young woman, who paid cash and gave her name as Norton. Apparently she was blonde too.'

'Before we go off to meet Mrs Walmsley, I've got a call to make.' Without explaining further, Jo went to the payphone and rang Vaz, hoping he wouldn't be at lunch.

He didn't sound all that pleased to hear from her. 'I knew you'd be in touch again,' he said. 'Luckily this isn't a bad moment, as I'm on my own. You realize my career prospects could be as dismal as Cass's after this, don't you?'

'You mean you've found something?'

'I think so,' he said cautiously. 'But I need to get at some more information this afternoon. Cass rang. She remembered certain files Sean didn't want the auditors to see. I'm going to try and find them and meet you both at Ponti's at half-past six. Cass knows where it is.'

'You'd better tell me because I'll meet you both there.'

Vaz explained and she wrote down the details. As Cass's phone was out of order, she added, 'If Cass calls again, tell her to hold on to that address book.'

'I think she will.' Vaz's voice became more formal. 'OK, thank you for calling. Goodbye.'

Macy was finishing off a plate of chips when Jo

rejoined him. He offered her some but she couldn't face even one. Her headache had eased but her stomach still felt queasy.

'Tell me about Cass and this mysterious address book on our way to the car,' Macy said. 'Why do you think it's so important?'

It was raining again outside and they walked briskly. 'Because as soon as Sean knew Cass had got hold of the book, he closed all the accounts listed in the back and got her sacked,' Jo replied, slightly out of breath.

'Why didn't he just ask her to give the book back? Or somehow make her give it back? Wouldn't that have been simpler?'

Jo felt her damp hair, which she knew would be going hopelessly curly. 'Maybe getting the book back wouldn't have made any difference. Once Cass had seen it, Sean feared she would be able to work out for herself what he was up to – as she worked at the bank. That's why he had to get rid of her.'

'But we don't know what this fiddle was?' Macy got in the car and Jo waited in the rain while he leant over and opened the passenger door.

'No, but Vaz – he works at the bank – is trying to find out. Cass was sure Nick helped Sean get her the sack, which could mean he's involved in the same business. Or maybe Sean could force Nick into helping – had some sort of hold over him, perhaps.' Jo paused, feeling quite pleased with this theory.

'Could be,' Macy agreed grudgingly. 'Either way it gives Nick Walmsley a wonderful reason for wanting Sean to disappear for ever. We're getting to the stage where we could hand this over to the police. They could do the donkey work then.'

The Walmsleys lived on a main road leading out of St Albans. The house was one of a line of uninspiring just-about-detached houses which were built on an embankment with their front lawns sloping steeply down to the road. Jo was looking up and trying to read the numbers when Macy braked sharply to avoid hitting a car which stopped in front of him. It was a near miss on the wet road with the rusty bumper of Macy's old Cortina finishing inches from the back of a shiny new Metro. He was about to pull away, swearing, when Jo told him not to bother.

'This is it. Number 96. We're here.' She stared up at the respectable, double-fronted 1950s house with its tidy white-painted windows and gable. Then she noticed the two women getting out of the Metro in front. The shorter one in low heels and a pink trench coat looked familiar.

Jo put her hand on Macy's arm. 'That's Carol, Nick's secretary.' Carol was looking guiltily at them as she locked up the car.

'Sorry,' she mimed with a rueful grin, 'forgot to signal.' She waved her left arm in a rough approximation of a hand signal. The other woman, older and not dressed for rain, waited patiently on the pavement.

'That must be Nick's wife,' Jo said when she saw the older woman was holding house keys. 'What are these two doing together?'

'Shall we say hello?' Macy suggested, opening the car door.

Carol's smile became more anxious when she saw Macy get out. 'Sorry. My fault entirely,' she said hurriedly. 'No damage done though—' She stopped when she saw Jo and for the second time that day, Jo enjoyed the dramatic effect she made simply by making an appearance.

'Oh, hello. We met at the bank yesterday,' Carol said, confused. 'What a coincidence.'

'Well, not really,' Jo explained, 'I wasn't a genuine candidate for the job. Actually we're private investigators and we've come to see if we can have a quick word with Mrs Walmsley?'

'With me?' This came out almost as a squawk from the woman who had been standing watching. She was trying ineffectually to pull her summer blazer round her to keep off some of the rain.

Carol stared at them. 'Good grief. Well, you meet all sorts. I suggest we all go in out of the rain – if that's all right with you, Mrs Walmsley?'

'I suppose so,' the other woman said unhappily and led the way up the path. Jo and Macy exchanged a quick amused glance and followed. 'Although I don't know what Nick's going to say about it all,' Mrs Walmsley said as they trooped down her hall.

'No, neither do I,' Jo heard Carol mutter under her breath.

'It's all right,' Macy said at his most reassuring, 'we've only just come from speaking to Nick and he knows that we're looking into Sean Fitzpatrick's death. I'm David Macy by the way,' he held out his hand, 'and this is Jo Hughes.'

'Lynne Walmsley.' She shook hands weakly, her worried eyes darting from one to the other. Her mascara was smudged and her face was pale and doubtful under over-dyed brown hair.

'Carol Forrest,' the younger woman said, nodding briefly at Jo and Macy, 'and now we've got the introductions out of the way, may I suggest a cup of tea? If you show me where the kitchen is, Mrs W., I'll make it while you go and sit down. And I think you were going to take a tablet, weren't you? Should I fetch one for you?'

'Oh, if you wouldn't mind,' Lynne said, giving in easily as if she was used to being looked after. 'The kitchen's through there and the tablets are in the drawer nearest the door. I'd be so grateful.' She turned to Jo and Macy and smiled wanly. 'You'd better come and sit down, I suppose.'

She showed them into the front room, which was furnished in a conservative but comfortable style. She took off her damp blazer and sank down on to one of the armchairs.

Still slightly mystified but enjoying herself, Jo sat next

to Macy on the sofa. 'Are you all right?' she asked politely as Lynne sat back and closed her eyes.

'Oh, yes, yes,' Lynne said without opening them, 'I've just had a very, very bad day. That's all. I don't know why I did it. It's a good job that woman has a heart after all.'

Carol entered the room during this speech but seemed unabashed. She tapped Lynne's arm lightly and held out a tablet and a glass of water. Lynne accepted both wordlessly. 'Tea won't be long,' Carol said bracingly.

'I'll feel better in a minute,' Lynne said, smiling at Jo and Macy reassuringly, as if this must be their biggest concern.

Macy cleared his throat. 'Mrs Walmsley, I expect the police have spoken to you about where your husband was when Sean Fitzpatrick died.'

'Yes, a policewoman took a statement yesterday. I must admit I thought that would be the end of it. But I should have known.' She sighed and laid her head back, closing her eyes again. 'Nick, Nick, Nick. He's the bane of my existence. I don't know what's up with him. He's not sleeping. He's never here. I don't know what to do.' Lynne finished on a low wail and sat up, scrabbling for her handkerchief.

Fortunately Carol came back just then pushing the teapot, cups and saucers on a trolley. 'You're not upsetting yourself again, are you? Pour yourself a cup of tea, you'll feel better.'

Lynne looked at Carol anxiously over the tea things. 'You won't tell him, will you? It's just going to make things worse if he knows I went to the bank to see you.'

Carol poured herself some tea. 'I won't say a word,' she promised, 'we all make mistakes.'

'Why did you go to the bank?' Jo asked patiently.

'To find out what was going on.' Lynne sat back with her cup and saucer. 'I had to know what he was up to.

But now I'm no wiser' – her face creased up again – 'I thought—'

'She thought he was having an affair with me,' Carol put in with a little self-conscious laugh.

'You don't deny you cover up for him when I ring. You always say he's at meetings. Who has meetings at eight o'clock at night, I want to know?' Lynne said, her voice rising.

'We've been through this,' Carol said soothingly, 'I've admitted I do tell porkies on his behalf. It's part of a PA's job to cover up for her boss. But I don't always know where he goes.'

'You mean he goes out of the office? These nights when you're working late?' Jo asked.

Carol looked guilty. She sipped her tea. 'Well, yes. Now and again. I told you I do half his work, didn't I?' she added defensively.

'But, Carol, you may be covering up for something really important—'

Jo was interrupted by Lynne, who suddenly banged her cup down. 'But who is he having an affair with? I know there's someone. I've found her clothes in a suitcase. I know he's going to leave me, I know—'

'What suitcase?' Macy asked in calm tones. He succeeded in distracting her.

She brought her brimming eyes to his. 'He's got his lover's clothes in there,' she said miserably.

'Show me.' Macy put down his cup and saucer and stood up. 'Come on,' he added encouragingly.

'All right.' Lynne got to her feet. 'Come with me. I'm not making it up, you know.'

Jo had been hoping for a quiet word with Carol but Lynne insisted that all four of them went upstairs. The main bedroom was dominated by a large double bed covered by a white quilt and lace pillows. Lynne slid back one of the wardrobe doors and took out a cream leather suitcase.

'I found this locked in the boot of his car,' she said in low tones. 'He's not the only one who can't sleep. The difference is I've never been a good sleeper. The other night I waited until he'd finally dropped off. I took his keys and searched his car. I knew if there was anything he didn't want me to see, that's where he'd keep it. I never go in his car you see unless I'm with him. I don't drive.' She placed the suitcase on the bed and took a key from a bedside drawer. 'I got this off his key ring.' She added, unlocking the case, 'God help me when he finds out. He'll definitely leave me.'

'But why did you suddenly become suspicious?' Jo asked curiously.

'I told you. He's been acting oddly. Staying out even later than usual' – she shot a look at Carol, who was standing at the back – 'at work, he said.'

Lynne opened the suitcase, which was crammed with women's clothes. It was packed reasonably neatly but the very fact it was so full meant the top layer had become disordered. The lace of a camisole dripped over the side, some smoky grey knickers lay on top and below them, what looked like a lemon slip. The heavier fabric of a dress or coat could be seen underneath.

'He must be planning to run off with her,' Lynne said gazing down at the clothes tearfully.

Jo looked over at Carol, who was peering at the contents of the case from a distance. Her face registered surprise and then two high spots of colour appeared on her cheeks. Macy sifted through the layers of clothes gently. 'Can I unpack some of them?' he asked Lynne.

'Go ahead,' she sighed, 'I've been through it all. There's no name on anything. Nothing personal.'

Macy laid some of the clothes on the bed in neat piles and shook out a heavy jacket, which had been at the bottom. He held it up for Jo to see. It was well made and distinctive in red and white leather.

'Well, I must get back to work,' Carol's practical voice

came from behind them. 'If you're all right now, Mrs W.?'

'I'll show you out,' Jo offered quickly, following Carol out of the room. 'What's going on?' she hissed in Carol's ear as they went downstairs. 'You know, don't you? Whose clothes are they? Not yours?'

They reached the hall and Carol headed for the front door. 'No. I've really no idea. He used to ask me to cover for him while he went out once a week. To meet someone – or a different lot of someones – I never asked.'

'But why lie for him? And to the police too?'

Carol opened the door and looked out at the steady rain. 'As I said, it's part of my job. Also his career is my career – at least partly – and he's doing well. When the police asked me, I automatically covered up for Nick. On Friday nights he always went out about six and I stayed on at work. It's just a coincidence that Sean happened to die on a Friday. Nick's been going out on Friday evenings for the last three years and the man wouldn't harm a fly. I know him.'

'But you don't know what he does on Friday nights,' Jo pointed out reasonably.

'It's none of my business. But I know he doesn't go swanning up the M1 to kill his best friend. For one thing, he always leaves his car at work and it was there that night too when I left.' Carol sighed impatiently. 'I can see it all seems odd to you, that I have such loyalty to my boss and to the bank. Especially when there's no sex involved. But I'm like that. I'd rather be at work than at home, to be honest. I'd rather be number-crunching for that weekly report than half-dead of boredom in front of the telly. Nick's just a good boss and his Friday nights off are nothing to do with me.' Carol gathered her trench coat around her, gave Jo a last pitying look and stepped out into the rain.

Jo watched her get into her car and turned to see Macy and Lynne coming down the stairs. He was obviously preparing to leave.

'Will you be all right?' Jo asked Lynne as the other woman looked tired and depressed.

'I'm going to my mother's,' she said stoutly. 'I'll pack a bag so I can stay overnight. It's not far – just two stops on the Tube.'

'If you pack quickly, I'll give you a lift there,' Macy offered.

Lynne looked pleased and went back upstairs to get ready. Jo was relieved. The woman seemed so volatile, she would have worried about leaving her on her own, but she couldn't help a quick glance at her watch. She hoped she was going to get to Ponti's on time to meet Vaz and Cass.

Macy seemed to have invited himself along to the meeting with Vaz and by the time they had found somewhere to park, there was little chance to argue. They had to hurry between late, straggling commuters. Even so they were fifteen minutes late.

The café was almost empty. It was a dark, narrow place, which mainly catered to lunch-time trade. While Jo bought two espressos at the counter, she peered into the back of the room and recognized Vaz and Cass, heads close together over a small table. Jo and Macy carried their coffees over and neither Cass nor Vaz noticed them until Jo was virtually at Cass's elbow. Jo apologized for being late and introduced Macy and the other two shifted along the bench seat so all four could squash round the table.

'So what could you find out from those account numbers?' Jo asked as soon as they were settled.

Vaz, still exquisitely smart but looking tired, was drinking a glass of milk. He stopped smiling at Cass and turned to Jo. 'I'm afraid you're probably right about Sean.'

'Why? What was he doing?'

Vaz whipped up his milk with a straw. 'Those accounts. I've been looking at them all day in my spare minutes. At first I couldn't see it. The only odd thing about them was that they were all closed within a short time of each other. They all had fairly large sums going in and coming out on a daily basis. That's a bit unusual but it wouldn't make an auditor raise his eyebrows.'

Vaz's eyes flickered back to Cass but he kept to the point. 'Then I tried to look for the files which Cass mentioned. I could only find two – I didn't have all that much time to look – but the forms for opening the account were missing on one and on the other were unclear. I think Sean must have set them up on the computer without proper authorization so that means they could be false accounts. Then I noticed that they were linked to real accounts.'

'What does that mean?' Jo asked.

'Linked accounts are like a current and deposit account belonging to the same person,' Cass put in unexpectedly. 'Or if someone is paying off a personal loan to another bank customer – like their mother or something – their accounts would be linked. It means money can be transferred from one to the other easily.'

'So Sean had made up false accounts and linked them to real ones so he could get money out of the real ones?' Jo worked it out aloud.

'Yes, basically,' Vaz agreed. 'The clever way he did it was to take money from an account at the start of business, put it in one of his false accounts, invest it on the stock market and return the money at the close of business. The customer lost a day's interest every time he did it but otherwise would be none the wiser.'

'Do you think Nick Walmsley knew about this?' Jo asked.

'I think someone else must have helped him and Nick would be the obvious person because Nick would have had to cover up for him.' Vaz turned back to Cass. 'At least this might mean you get your job back. It's hard to believe it of Sean, though, isn't it? I thought he was just interested in having a good time.'

'How far was Nick involved, do you think?' Macy asked.

Vaz lifted his shoulders elegantly. 'Equally guilty, but I would guess Sean did the dirty work of switching the money from one account to another. Sean set up the system, I imagine, and from what I can see, he's been running it for at least two years. Nick would have had to turn a blind eye at the right moments and sign the transfer forms. And help keep the auditors at bay.'

'Actually it's hard to see what was in it for Nick,' Cass put in. 'He's well known for being ambitious and this would bring his career to a full stop for—'

'Money,' Macy finished.

'Yes, but I bet Sean talked him into it,' Cass persevered, 'or maybe he could somehow force Nick to go along with the idea.'

'Once Nick found out what Sean was doing and didn't say anything, he would be just as implicated as Sean,' Vaz observed. 'That in a way would give Sean a hold over him. What do you want me to do with this information?'

'Whatever you think you should,' Jo advised. 'Tell your boss for a start, I suppose.'

'We're going to tell the police about it as soon as possible,' Macy said. 'Are you willing to give us the address book, Cass? To show them.'

As Cass handed it over a little reluctantly, Vaz was looking at her admiringly. 'It was Cass telling me about those files that finally completed the picture,' he said. 'I hope you get your job back. You ought to,' he added to her.

'Doubt it,' she said philosophically, 'but at least they might be persuaded to give me a decent reference now. Thanks to you.'

Jo could see that her own and Macy's presence was superfluous. She thanked Vaz for helping and made an excuse to leave. Macy acquiesced and they went out into the stuffy evening air together.

Chapter Seventeen

'Who was Nick's lover?' Jo wondered aloud as they walked back to Macy's car. The rain had stopped hours ago but the clouds remained and the air was stale and heavy with petrol fumes.

'Why not Carol?' Macy suggested. 'She told one lie about Nick's whereabouts. Why not a bigger lie?'

'I don't think so.' Jo shook her head, thinking of her conversation with Carol on the Walmsleys' doorstep. 'She convinced me, anyway. I think this is a triangular puzzle and we're only looking at two corners of it. We've got the partnership between Sean and Nick. Taurus and Scorpio. The materialistic bull was outwitted by the ambitious scorpion but there has to be someone else—'

'What are you rambling on about?' Macy demanded as they reached the car.

'Nick is Scorpio. I asked Lynne when I was trying to hurry her to pack her overnight bag. Scorpio is the opposite sign to Taurus and for ruthlessness, they beat Taurus every time.'

Macy looked bemused. 'I don't know about you but I need something to eat. I can't do all this work on an empty stomach.' He got into the car. 'Let's go and eat. I'll pay.'

'You don't have to pay—' Jo began automatically. Someone had once told her that her determination not to be obliged to anyone amounted to an obsession. But it didn't stop her.

'See it as part of your expenses,' Macy interrupted impatiently. 'And I won't consult you about the restaurant, does that make you feel any better?'

Jo started to argue but gave up. She could see Macy wasn't listening anyway.

'More and more I think this is out of our hands. Tomorrow I'm going to see Debbie,' he said distractedly as he waited to join traffic on the main road. 'There's only so much we should keep from the police and I think we're about to cross the line into their territory.'

'But we've probably crossed it already,' Jo argued. 'And what about Connor? What will we tell him?'

'What we know,' Macy said succinctly. 'We've earned our crust as far as he's concerned. He's not expecting us to make him a present of his brother's murderer trussed up and ready for justice. I've a good idea Nick Walmsley must have got rid of Sean—'

'We have no evidence. We know he had a good reason to. We don't know where he was between five o'clock and eleven that night. But we have nothing to tie him to the actual murder. His car was at the bank, too, don't forget.'

'Details. The police will sort them out. They ought to know all this stuff about the fraud Nick and Sean were running.'

'There's still an awful lot we don't know,' Jo maintained, nettled. Why did conversations with Macy usually make her irritable, she wondered? He was always overlooking important details when it suited him. She was sorry she had agreed to eat with him. In any case, she thought, as they passed a sign to the M4, he probably had a motorway service area in mind.

'All right,' he was saying with excessive patience, 'we know Nick Walmsley must have had something to do with this scam of Sean's.' He turned into a dusty side street and slowed down to pass a line of parked cars.

'Vaz seemed to think it was certain. If so, then why

would Nick kill Sean? It wouldn't have been very sensible,' Jo pointed out, 'goose and golden egg and all that.'

His choice of restaurant was a Spanish one on the corner of a run-down residential street. There were plastic vine leaves and empty wine bottles strung up outside. To Jo it looked the kind of place where the food had to be wonderful or it would never have kept going. She and Macy took the only empty table, which was squashed between the wall and a couple who were sitting gazing at each other in adoring silence.

'We know Nick lied to the police about his whereabouts on Friday night,' Macy went on, 'I can't see why you're coming to his defence now.'

'I'm not. It's just that we're missing something obvious,' Jo insisted. To ignore important details would offend any Virgo and Jo was determined to work out whatever it was they had overlooked. 'I'm sure there's someone else involved.'

'You mean this woman in the lay-by. Could be Nick's lover?' Macy paused to consult the menu.

'Why did he have her clothes?' Jo frowned, following her own train of thought. 'Something is really bothering me about that.' They had to break off their conversation to order some food. 'You saw the jacket she wore. Was there any blood on it?' she asked.

'It looked clean to me but blood would wash off the leather reasonably easily.'

'So why keep it? If Nick knew his girlfriend had worn it to do in his old chum, then why keep the jacket?' Jo sat back while the waiter poured out two glasses of red wine. 'Do you think Rosie is Nick's lover?'

'She was the bait, do you mean? Nick's accomplice. She got Sean to that pub in the middle of nowhere, then left and phoned him to say her car had broken down. Sean drives to help her and gets walloped over the head by Nick. Or by Rosie herself, I suppose. But Rosie has an alibi – of sorts.' Macy sighed. 'These are avenues the police can go down. We have enough to tell our client. That's what concerns me.' Macy came to a halt due to the arrival of his lamb and Jo's paella.

'And what about the suitcase of women's clothes?' Jo went on after a couple of mouthfuls. 'Are they Rosie's? The underwear was all size sixteen. Too big for Rosie. The girl we met at the Royal Shakespeare Theatre was only a twelve at most.'

'And there's the car.' Macy refilled her glass. 'It sounds like the car was bought by the same girl who was in the lay-by. But why would they need a car? Nick had one of his own.'

'Too obvious,' Jo said. She could see Macy was coming round to her point of view, that the problems were far from solved. But still she could not move him from his decision to go to the police.

'I don't want us to get in too deep,' he said, 'Sean was involved in some sort of fraud, which I don't think we understand. And I don't like the sound of his druggy pals.' Macy paused to clear his plate. 'What do you think of the food here?'

Jo left off trying to persuade him for the time being and gave her opinion on her meal, which had been very good, from what she could remember. When they left the restaurant, she noticed that the couple at the next table looked distinctly disappointed.

'I think they were fascinated from the first mention of murder. After that they hardly looked at each other,' she told Macy cheerfully on the way to the car.

'I'm not surprised. Violent death is a lot more interesting than true love,' Macy remarked lugubriously.

On the journey back Jo came up with another loose end for Macy to consider. 'I don't see how it could have been Rosie who bought the Chevette. She told us she couldn't drive.'

'You're so good at thinking up these questions, why don't you come up with some answers now and again?'

Macy responded grumpily. As usual with him, conversation died out when they couldn't find any more to say about the case. They spent most of the journey back to Coventry in silence. Jo was planning how she would get hold of Rosie tomorrow when Macy stopped the car outside her house.

'Do you think I deserve a coffee?' he asked, to Jo's surprise. He was looking across at her, his hands still on the wheel. Ready to leave in case I say no, Jo thought. He looked ruffled, tired and attractive.

'OK,' Jo agreed, secretly pleased that Macy had chosen to unbend even this much. She led the way indoors, opened the door of her flat and was met by Preston, butting her legs with his large ginger head and wailing. The light on the answering machine was flashing and Preston demanded food.

'If you feed the cat, I'll play your messages back and get the coffee,' Macy offered, following her in.

Jo put down her keys and paused before switching the light on. The cat and the phone could wait a second, she thought. She turned to Macy so he was close and put up a hand to the back of his neck, where his hair was very soft. He looked at her seriously a minute before he kissed her. And Jo was glad afterwards she had at least enjoyed one good kiss that night.

She only turned back to Preston when his pathetic wails could not be ignored any longer. She went to the kitchen to deal with the cat while Macy switched on most of the lights. She opened a can of cat food and collected Preston's bowls from the balcony while the cat slowed down the proceedings by winding himself around her legs and generally getting in the way. She could hear Macy in the other room rewinding the answering machine. Then she heard the click of the play button.

'Jo, it's Nick,' came a disembodied voice distorted by the poor quality of the tape, 'I hope you don't mind me ringing you at home. I got your number from your application form. I've been thinking about what you said at lunch time and I'd like to talk to you about it. I'm coming to Coventry tonight. Can you meet me? I'll ring you again when I get there.'

'He didn't say what time that was,' Macy remarked, appearing in the kitchen doorway. 'And your answer phone is too primitive to record the time of calls.'

The machine clicked and went into a second message. This was a woman's voice, bright and cheerful. 'It's Kelly Greenaway. Your jacket is fixed, Jo, and you can pick it up any time. Have you had time to look at my chart yet? What about a consultation at my house soon?' Kelly then left her number and address.

'That's just some astrology work. I've been re-interpreting her chart,' Jo said, pleased that Macy had evidence that her other line of business was still thriving. 'I told you about Kelly. Did you ever remember where you'd heard of her—?'

Nick's voice interrupted her. This message sounded more urgent and almost pleading. 'It's Nick again. Please could you come down to the Castaway tonight? You know where it is. I'll be there until late. It's really important that I speak to you. Try and come.'

Jo looked at Macy, who was frowning, his eyes seeming darker than usual. When he looked up, she read his resigned expression and knew her plans for the night were not going to materialize.

'What do you want to do?' he asked as if he had not already decided.

'It's ten to eleven. The pubs don't close till eleven. If he really is staying late, he should still be there. But as we've just decided that Nick's a murderer I'm not daft enough to go on my own. You'll have to come with me.'

'Of course we should go to the police first,' Macy said. 'But whatever we do, we'd better get a move on. The bozo didn't leave any times on his messages and I don't suppose he'll wait for ever.'

'We'll call the police from the pub,' Jo suggested. They left Preston to his dinner and hurried outside to Macy's car, where the seats were still warm. Jo glanced at him as he started the engine and wondered if she had guessed right when she assumed he would want to try and meet Nick. There was a keen sense of disappointment in the air but it was not only that which made her suddenly feel low. From nowhere a feeling of pessimism hit her and she felt sure she and Macy had made the wrong decision.

Chapter Eighteen

'He must think I've got the address book,' Jo remarked to Macy when they were speeding along narrow lanes towards the Castaway.

'Very likely,' was Macy's terse reply as he braked to avoid a cyclist. Once or twice he had to pull in to allow other cars to pass. Jo peered vainly at them in case she recognized Nick but it was difficult to distinguish the drivers in the dark.

'I thought he was worried when I mentioned it at lunch time,' Jo said, speaking her thoughts aloud. 'I sort of implied I had it because I didn't want him to go to Cass for it.'

Macy didn't respond. As they approached the pub, there were a few people hanging around their cars, preparing to leave, but the pub itself was closed. Macy rapped on the door while Jo watched the last few people drive away.

'He's not here,' she said, her cheerfulness sounding patently false to her ears. She walked up to have a look at the only two cars that were left. They probably belonged to the bar staff, she thought. 'He must have left,' she called over her shoulder to Macy, who was heading round the back of the pub.

The night was clammy and black and she resisted the temptation to get back in Macy's car. She noticed something glinting against the driver's door and realized he had left his keys in the lock. She removed them, keeping them in her hand as she walked across the silent car park. Feeling nervous and not quite sure what she was looking for, she was nevertheless turning over recent events in her mind. Finding Macy's keys had started her worrying about missing details again.

Why should the idea of locking things away – personal property – keep niggling her? There was the suitcase which had been locked in Nick's car boot. Lynne Walmsley had taken the key out of a bedside drawer to open it. Jo's feet came to a halt in the lane. Suddenly she saw the questions and answers as if they were written across her retina.

How had Lynne been able to unlock the case? Because she had taken the key off Nick's key ring. But if the suitcase belonged to his lover, why would Nick have the key? And on his key ring? Surely it would be more natural to keep it separate. Wasn't it more likely the suitcase was his? And the clothes. Which would explain the large sizes.

Jo remembered Carol's face when she saw the underclothes: she had looked as if she had just put two and two together. And of course if Nick had been dressed as a woman to kill Sean, then maybe he wouldn't need an accomplice. Jo walked slowly, letting this sink in. At first it seemed very dark and quiet but she began to make out a bass thumping in the distance and the occasional shout, as if there was a party going on somewhere. She looked round her at the empty lane with fields beyond and couldn't imagine where. But it was the kind of still night when sound carries a long way.

Jo realized she was near where Alan had met her in his car last Friday. She looked over her shoulder again but couldn't see Macy. She walked slowly, her low heels sounding loud on the tarmac, towards the track which led to the reservoir. She felt ridiculously tense and wanted to be able to give up this idea with dignity and return to her flat, saying, 'Ah well, we tried. Now let's go to bed.'

She smiled to herself at this idea. As she looked up, her eye caught something pale in the bushes below to her right. Down towards the reservoir, she saw the front wing and side of a light-coloured car, some distance away and half hidden. It must be parked on the track. She moved a few paces forward, with her heart hammering away pointlessly, and came to the gate she remembered. From here she could no longer see the car. The gate was open, despite a notice saying the land belonged to the water authority, but Jo hesitated. Was Nick parked down there? If so God knows what he was doing. Or had he left his car? In which case—?

Behind her rapid footsteps were coming along the lane. Ridiculously, she looked at the nearby bushes and thought of hiding. She stepped to the side of the lane, where she did not feel so vulnerable, her feet finding soft damp grass. After a minute, she was relieved to see it was Macy walking quickly towards her, hands in pockets. She stepped out so as not to startle him but her appearance still brought him up short. He swore feelingly when he saw it was her.

'Ssh, I've seen a car,' she murmured, 'on the track by the lake.' It was too dark to see Macy's face but she felt him sigh.

'Oh, God. Better go and have a look then,' he said, sounding heavy-hearted.

They passed through the gate, with Jo slightly ahead. As soon as they turned off the lane, the night seemed to close in and the beat of the music that Jo had noticed before seemed louder. The track sloped quite steeply down and because they couldn't see much, the gravel felt slippy and uncertain. Behind her Jo heard Macy slither once or twice.

The car was parked at the last twist of the lane before the reservoir. The first thing Jo noticed was that the driver's door wasn't closed properly. The lines of the metallic silver body caught what little light there was. Behind the car she could see the reservoir, flat and black, almost still. The rock music was distinct now and she suddenly remembered the club house and realized there must be a party going on there. Perhaps Nick had gone to that, she thought whimsically.

But as they got closer to the car, Jo could see someone sitting in the driving seat. Involuntarily she came to a halt, knowing she must be in full view. The driver didn't seem to move and the dread that had made her nervous earlier came back full force. She made her legs start moving forward again.

Before she went up to the car, she was sure it was Nick. From his shoulders, the rounded cheek and the pale hair, he was recognizable as the man she had chatted to at lunch time. As she got closer, she was sure he was dead. His hands were resting on the steering-wheel. But there was a total stillness about him which convinced her. She saw he was slumped forward, his mouth was open and his eyes strangely protruding.

'Shit,' she heard herself say and Macy was following so close he almost walked into her.

'Don't touch anything. We'll get the police,' Macy said softly and added, 'Sod it. I wish we had a torch.' He walked around the car to the passenger side. Disregarding his own advice, he opened the passenger door and the interior light came on.

Jo stood very close to the body, unable to do anything but watch. Nick looked as smart as he had when he had left the pub in Richmond. This struck her as odd, almost indecent. Looking at him disturbed her but she couldn't seem to drag her eyes away. He looked not exactly peaceful but unharmed. There was no blood or sign of injury. And yet he was definitely dead.

Taking a breath, Jo pulled her sleeve over her hand so as not to leave any marks and opened the driver's door, which was already ajar. She still could see no sign of how he had died. Her first thought was a heart attack or some other seizure. But would the body be this neat, sitting upright and apparently calm? She could smell something strange in the car, a faintly medicinal smell, like disinfectant.

'They keys are in the ignition, doors and boot unlocked. I can't understand it,' Macy said quietly from behind her. Jo stood up and gently pushed the door to again. She still couldn't take her eyes off the body. From the lake someone shouted. Jo leapt away from the car, jarring her whole body. The shout was followed by a scream and then a splash.

'Sounds like kids,' Macy commented calmly but Jo noticed he was breathing fast as well. There was another loud splash from behind them followed by raucous shouting and laughter. 'I wonder if they heard anything. The police will find out. We'd better ring them.' Macy sounded weary.

They walked back in silence towards the pub. While they passed the car, Jo kept her eyes on the ground, almost afraid that if she looked at Nick's body, she would become transfixed again. Even in the dark she noticed the gravel around the car was churned up, particularly at the back. She thought maybe Nick had manoeuvred the car before parking but the marks were not consistent all the way around. It looked more like there had been a scuffle behind the car. Jo puzzled over this: Nick had looked too neat for a man who had just been in a fight.

'Must be a natural death, do you think?' she wondered aloud. 'A heart attack or a fit?'

'There would be more mess,' Macy said succinctly from behind her.

'Suicide then? He took an overdose and drove here to die?'

'More likely. Still should be more mess though. I think death is usually pretty messy.'

They turned on to the lane. 'But why arrange to meet me and then kill himself?' Jo said.

'Stop worrying about how he died, we'll call the police and they'll be here in a minute.'

It was not the kind of problem which was so easily dismissed. Jo's mind kept returning to it throughout the long wait to be questioned by the police. The landlord, Matti, while not happy to have to leave his bed to let Macy and Jo in, gradually softened up as the hours ticked by. At first he had told them to wait in the darkened public bar while he went to phone the police. Then he grudgingly gave them a tot of cheap brandy. When Macy offered to pay, he scowled and refilled their glasses. After that he switched on the lights and produced a heater because it was surprisingly cold in the bar.

When the police arrived, Matti reappeared with a tray of hot drinks. The coffee was very strong and a lot more to Jo's taste than the brandy. A pale, tired-looking man in an overcoat told Jo and Macy to wait. Squad cars arrived outside and lit up the car park with sweeping orange light. Uniformed constables came in muttering and were sent out again by the man in the overcoat. After a long wait an unknown detective sergeant came over to question them and they were finally allowed to leave the pub at 3.30 a.m. with instructions to report to Inspector Cash at Coventry police station the next day. Jo and Macy went back to her flat. It seemed too late for Macy to go home so they both lay on her bed, only half-undressed, and slept a stupefied sleep until past nine when Jo awoke to the sound of the telephone ringing.

Chapter Nineteen

When she answered the phone Jo was greeted by a cheerful young constable reminding her that she was due at the police station, 'sooner rather than later, love'. As it was mainly due to the police that they had got in so late, Jo's assurance that she would be there as soon as possible was given through gritted teeth. Although Macy was still asleep in the bedroom, she saw no reason to account for his whereabouts. She put the phone down and went off to make coffee and shower.

In the shower it occurred to her that the police would be interested in the messages Nick had left on her answering machine. As soon as she was dressed she replayed the tape to see if it brought any enlightenment. Nick's voice was anxious, almost pleading, but Jo could not deduce anything else. She put the tape into an envelope to take with her to the police station. It would certainly not do any harm to have proof of why she and Macy were snooping around near the dead body last night.

She sat down with her coffee and tried to put the night's events out of her mind. The case was now with the police. There was this week's astrology column still to be written and she must arrange to see Kelly Greenaway. Jo found the comments she had typed on Kelly's chart and put them in a presentation folder. She rang Kelly and offered to deliver them late that afternoon, allowing plenty of time at the police station. Kelly suggested six o'clock because her daughter would be in bed by then. When this was settled Jo made a start on her weekly prediction column. She looked up the position of the planets for the coming week and saw that Mercury and Saturn had moved out of opposition so at least it should be an easier week than the last one. She had got as far as Leo when Macy appeared from the bedroom.

'There's coffee in the kitchen and plenty of hot water,' Jo said and Macy went robotically in the direction of the bathroom. Jo was working on Scorpio by the time he re-emerged looking more human. 'You don't want any breakfast, do you?' Jo asked discouragingly. 'The police have been on the phone and they want us to go down there as soon as possible.'

'I never eat breakfast,' Macy said as one stating an article of faith. 'But have you got any tea? I can't take any more coffee – I feel like I've been drinking it all night.'

Jo left her work to hunt for the teapot, something she only used when her mother visited. 'Do you think they'll keep us long at the police station?' she asked from under the sink.

'Well, yes – if last night is anything to go by. I think they're a bit bemused by Nick's death—' Macy sat hunched over her kitchen table.

'Last night I heard the Inspector say it must be a heart attack.' She filled the kettle and started searching for the tea bags.

'They'll be asking for a post-mortem anyway but I doubt if they'll know the outcome yet. This morning they will just want us to run through why we think Nick killed Sean, which will mean explaining all that stuff about the fraud at the bank—'

'Will you mention the women's clothes?' Jo had a look in the fridge in case there was anything in there which she could offer Macy. There was a lump of cheese and an out-of-date yoghurt. She closed the door again.

'Yes, there's no point in keeping things back. See what *they* make of it.' Macy added with some relish: 'We'll explain about the address book too because that makes it clear not only what Nick was doing at the Castaway but what we were doing there.'

'That means involving Cass,' Jo pointed out worriedly.

'She's already involved.'

Jo saw that Macy's instinct for self-preservation was as strong as ever. She poured him a cup of tea and went to collect her astrology work together. No doubt there would be hours of waiting at the police station and she would get a chance to finish it there.

'How is it going? The zodiac stuff? Are you doing consultations now?' Macy asked, watching her through the kitchen doorway.

Jo explained about Kelly Greenaway. It would be one of the few private consultations she had ever given as most of her work tended to be done by post. 'And Kelly's a really interesting character,' she went on, 'I've remembered why she seemed familiar when I met her—'

'Yes, you mentioned it and I went back to the office and looked it up. Her kid was kidnapped, wasn't she?'

The kidnapping had been a big local news story about a year ago and it had come back to Jo when she was working on Kelly's chart. 'The little girl was only about two. But they got her back, didn't they? And she was unscathed.'

Macy nodded. He took a professional interest in local crime. 'They found the kid in a caravan near Bedworth with some weirdo. Of course the Greenaways are rolling in money. Well, Mark Greenaway is. They stumped up the ransom.'

'That's right. It's fascinating because all this is in Kelly's chart.' Jo continued enthusiastically, 'There are definite indications of dramatic family upheavals. It's unusual to have the sun and moon both in the eighth house. And the influence of Pluto is very strong.' She glanced up and saw Macy's eyes had a glazed look. She also noticed that he had finished his tea so she changed the subject and told him her theory that Nick was a transvestite. 'He could have been the person in the lay-by.'

Macy looked at her doubtfully. 'I suppose from the back, bending over the bonnet of a car, he might be mistaken for a woman,' he mused. 'But that still doesn't explain why he would keep the clothes—'

'Because they weren't just the clothes he did the murder in. They were his outfits.'

'Possibly. Come on, let's go and dump these problems on the police.' Macy stood up, straightened his rumpled clothes and pronounced himself ready to go. He and Jo were on their way out of the flat when the phone rang. She answered it frostily, thinking it was another reminder from the police.

'Jo – is Macy with you?' Alan's voice sounded more than usually brusque. When Jo hesitated for a split second, he carried straight on, 'It's the only other place I can think of. I've tried his usual haunts—' Jo felt her eyebrows rising involuntarily at this but she did not interrupt. 'He'll throw a wobbly when he finds out: Connor Fitzpatrick's gone missing. His elder brother's just been on the phone. Connor's been gone since yesterday. Nobody knows where he is and his house has been turned over. What's more, he still owes us money.'

'Macy's here, you'd better speak to him.' Jo handed over the phone. Her first thought was that Sean's debtors had decided to carry out their threats.

Contrary to Alan's expectations, Macy's reaction was calm and mild.

He listened to Alan in silence most of the time, jotted down a phone number and promised to meet him at the office later. But he was frowning when he put the phone down. 'I hate it when something happens to one of our clients,' he said moodily, adding more briskly, 'Kieran Fitzpatrick called the office this morning. I suppose I'd better speak to him. Do you mind if I call him from here?'

'Go ahead,' Jo agreed, 'but could you ask him a favour for me?' Despite worrying about Connor, a handy solution to another little problem had occurred to her. 'Will you ask him to send us a photograph of Sean's wedding?'

Macy gave her a doubtful look but, characteristically, didn't give her the pleasure of explaining her theory. He simply picked up the phone and dialled the number he had written down. Jo heard him being quietly polite to Kieran. She guessed that the break-in at Connor's house had been done by the dealer who was owed money. Maybe his patience ran out and he was looking for things he could take instead. This idea seemed to be confirmed when Macy had finished the conversation. He told her that the TV, CD player, video and cash had been taken from Connor's house.

'Did Kieran promise to send the wedding photo?' Jo asked.

'No problem. He'll have it in the post tonight. He thinks I'm mad of course but—' Macy lifted his hands philosophically. 'We'd better go or they'll be sending a squad car for us.'

'I think Rosie could be the woman Sean married,' Jo explained on the way downstairs, unable to keep quiet about this theory any longer. 'She's got to fit in somewhere. Otherwise why did she meet him in the pub? And I'm sure she helped Nick kill him by phoning about the car breakdown. Although maybe she didn't know that was what Nick was going to do. Either way we should try and find her—'

'Maybe later if you like,' Macy sighed, 'depending on what the police say and what time we're finished at the station.'

In fact it was past four when Jo was told she could go.

The detective from the drugs squad who had been making her go over every detail of her late-night conversation with Connor told her Macy had left an hour ago. Jo only had a couple of hours before she had to go to Leamington to see Kelly but she was still determined to make an effort to find Rosie. The first thing to try was Rosie's phone number, which she had noted down and left in her car. She walked across to where she had parked it and was surprised to see Macy leaning against the passenger door.

'I went back to the office for a shower. Debbie said they would be finished with you in an hour or so. I thought you wanted to tie up this loose end and find Rosie? She's at the Midlands Dance Championships in Birmingham. If you want to drive us there, I'll tell you how I know.'

Jo felt slightly disgruntled to have the initiative taken away from her but she fell in with Macy's plans with a good grace. As she drove on to the ring-road, she pointed out that she would have to be in Leamington for six.

'Shouldn't be any problem.' Macy seemed in good spirits. 'I asked Alan to find out if there were any ballroom dancing competitions coming up. He used to go to lessons, you know.'

'I can imagine.'

'He rang up Rita, his old instructress, and she gave him a list of all the local competitions. I'm fairly sure that's where Rosie will be.'

'Yes – with Dean. I remember he mentioned the Midlands Championships. You'd better tell me where we're going.'

Chapter Twenty

The Baptist Central Hall was not easy to find and Jo had already made two U-turns before they finally arrived at the hall, which was a converted cinema surrounded by Indian restaurants. She followed Macy through double doors at the back of the foyer and was met by a small man in a black tie and dinner jacket, who was standing by a desk in the corridor.

'Are these the Midlands Dance Championships?' Macy asked.

'Yes, sir,' the man answered politely, smiling through a neat beard. 'Name, sir, please?' He consulted a book which was open on the desk in front of him. 'Are you a member?'

'We're from the *Birmingham Evening News*,' Macy said glibly. 'Down here, is it?' He started along the corridor and the smart bearded man did not object.

Jo paused to peer through the round windows in the old cinema doors at the end of the corridor. There was a stage and a small band at the far end of the large room. A cluster of overdressed young men and women were dancing in the space where the seats used to be. Other people stood around looking either bored or tense. She pushed open the doors and was met by a blast of music from the speakers. She and Macy walked past the dancers, who were flouncing up and down in time to the surprisingly raucous Latin American beat, the men thrusting out hairless chests.

'Half these are just kids,' Macy observed as he sidestepped to avoid a cerise skirt that stuck out two feet either side of the diminutive girl wearing it.

'Do you want a drink?' Jo asked. 'There's a bar over there.'

Macy agreed and they took their drinks to an unsteady table at the edge of the dance floor just as the music finished. The six or seven couples struck various attitudes and then tripped off the floor, clinging to each other's hands and smiling aggressively. While the smooth voice of an MC filled in the gap between dances, Jo looked around for Rosie and Dean.

'Excuse me, can I sit here a minute?' A woman flashed a smile at them over a low-cut black dress. 'It's just that I'm having trouble with my slingbacks.' She bent over and fiddled with one patent-leather shoe. She seemed older than a lot of the competitors and a thick leg showed through the slit in her dress. Macy asked if she knew where he could find Rosie Martell.

'Still in the dressing-room, I should think,' the woman said, trying to loosen the gold buckle, 'she'll be out for the tango in a minute if you hang on.' The MC called the next dancers to the floor and she gave Macy an encouraging smile. 'Might see you later.' She turned and hissed at her partner, who was hovering behind her, and they stepped on to the dance floor.

Jo noticed Dean first: distinctive, with his long parted hair, he was threading his way through a crowd of people near the bar. 'Here's Dean,' Macy murmured quietly, 'now where's Torvill?'

Rosie came into view from behind a pillar, holding on to Dean's frilly shirt sleeve. Macy must have caught her eye because she looked in their direction and away again quickly. Dean had stopped to speak to someone and she waited near him. After half a minute, she risked another look. Then she said something to Dean and started towards their table.

'What are you doing here?' she asked. Her wide eyes were challenging but her hands looked nervous. 'Taking an interest in the dancing, are you?'

'You remember us, then?' Macy stood up and pulled up a spare chair for her. 'Can we have a chat?'

'Not now,' Rosie said anxiously. 'We're due to go on next. Couldn't you choose a better time?'

'Nick Walmsley's dead,' Jo said by way of explanation.

Rosie was looking around for Dean. 'Who's he?'

'Sean's boss from the bank. You know that, don't you?' Jo went on determinedly.

'Never heard of him. And I don't know what you're after, but—'

'Just a talk.' Macy held her gaze. 'You said you didn't know Sean Fitzpatrick but your number was in his address book.'

Rosie's hands, which had been playing with a silk flower on her dress, suddenly became still and some of the nerve went out of her face. 'You what?' she said bluntly.

The dance was finishing and Dean came up looking worried. 'Come on, Rosie. This is no time to get stuck in conversation.' He looked at Jo and Macy irritably but apparently didn't remember them. Or didn't choose to. 'We're on now,' he muttered to Rosie.

'I'll stay here,' Macy said, sitting down and taking up his pint. 'Will you speak to me afterwards?'

Rosie gave them an uncertain look and Dean grabbed her hand. 'What the hell is going on?' He glared at Macy. 'If you've ballsed this up for us...' His sentence trailed off and he tugged Rosie towards the dance floor.

'You know Rosie's name isn't in Sean's address book,' Jo said mildly.

'That's true,' Macy agreed, taking a drink from his glass, 'but Rosie doesn't know what's in it.'

'I think she looks worried,' Jo said, watching her dance. 'Let's hope we can prise her away from Dean and get her to tell us what she knows.' She looked at her watch anxiously.

When they left the dance floor, Rosie turned towards them, still wearing a fixed smile, and mouthed, 'Five minutes.'

Jo tried to be patient while waiting for Rosie to appear. She came out eventually, having changed into a lurid strapless dress with a stiff skirt, and made her way to their table.

'How did you do?' Jo asked.

'Not bad at all, in the circumstances,' Rosie said frostily. Her face was still shiny with sweat after dancing. 'Dean's furious with you . . .' She held her long hair back from her face to cool down. Looking from Jo to Macy, she said, with the return of her usual cheek, 'Are you going to buy me a drink now?'

'All right,' Macy agreed, getting to his feet.

'Bacardi and Coke, please,' Rosie said sweetly. 'I can have one now we've finished the big number. What do you want, then?' she added to Jo when Macy had gone to the bar.

'Just for you to tell us what you were doing with Sean at the Castaway on June the eighteenth.'

'Or?' Rosie eyed her sulkily. 'What will you do if I don't tell you?'

'We'll take Sean's address book to the police.'

Rosie accepted the drink which Macy brought over. She took a mouthful and looked at them speculatively. 'I don't believe you for a minute. But I knew it'd have to come out. I'll tell you.' She got up, carrying her drink. 'Come on. We'll go outside where it's cooler.' Jo and Macy exchanged a glance and followed her.

'I did know Sean,' Rosie said matter of factly as she made her way towards a fire exit door, 'he used to come to Leamington on business about once a month – so he said. I met him at the club where I work part time. He took me out a few times – mainly to casinos and night clubs – it was quite good really.' She looked up at Macy as she leaned back on the metal bar to open the door.

'But . . .' Jo prompted. They followed her out into the car park, which was deserted.

'But he was just messing me about,' Rosie sighed. 'He would use my flat as somewhere to stay. It wasn't me he was interested in.' She found a wall to sit on. She sipped her drink and looked up at Macy hopefully. 'Ciggie?'

He produced a packet. Rosie took a cigarette and a light. 'You're a good listener,' she commented.

Macy shrugged. 'Part of the job.' He sat down next to her and lit a cigarette for himself. 'Tell me what you were doing in the Castaway.'

'Oh yes; well, you've got the picture about Sean and me, haven't you? He was getting fed up with me. What he didn't know is, I got pregnant.' Rosie looked at Jo and shook her head dismally, her long blonde hair falling in front of her face. She pushed it back again. 'My own stupid fault but still I held him partly responsible. By the time I knew for sure, Sean was hardly speaking to me. I still saw him at the club but he wasn't staying in my flat any more or taking me out. I knew he was loaded and I wanted him to pay for the abortion. I wanted it done privately – the best place I could . . .' She paused, looking down at the grimy pavement. 'This makes me sound awful, doesn't it?'

'No – just practical,' Jo said.

Rosie gave a laugh. 'Well, that wasn't what Sean said when I told him. First of all I had to find a way of getting him to talk to me in private—'

'Rosie! For God's sake – it's the formation number next,' Dean's anguished voice cut across the car park. He was leaning out of the fire escape door.

'Got to go,' Rosie said staunchly. She stubbed out her cigarette in the empty glass and waved to Dean.

'If we wait here, will you come back and tell us the rest?' Macy asked.

'Well, I've started so I may as well bloody finish.' Rosie grinned and hurried back indoors.

Jo sighed and looked at her watch. 'I can't wait,' she said, 'I mustn't miss my appointment with Kelly.' She felt guilty but she had promised herself that astrology business would not be sacrificed to PI work.

Macy shrugged. 'I'll wait here, then. It looks like she met Sean in the pub, doesn't it? But I doubt if she had any more to do with it than that.'

Jo was inclined to agree. 'How will you get back?' she asked to appease her conscience.

'Train, I suppose. Don't worry, I won't be helpless without you.'

Jo didn't argue. As she walked to her car, she wondered uncharitably if Macy was staying behind because he fancied Rosie. This didn't occupy her for long though as there were more important things to worry her. She knew she would have to drive fast to get to Kelly's on time.

Macy, on the other hand, was in no hurry. He sat where he was and finished his cigarette. It wasn't long before Rosie came out, carrying another drink and trailing a turquoise ostrich feather.

'Where was I?' she said, taking her place on the wall beside him.

'You were trying to get a word with Sean in private.'

'Oh, yes. I probably would never have seen him again but he couldn't keep away from the club. He was mad about my boss. Although she couldn't be bothered with him.'

'Hang on – I'm lost. What's this club?'

'Sorry, I'm rabbiting on, aren't I? This is the sports club where I work that I'm on about now. Kelly's my boss. She owns the place.'

'Who?' Macy interrupted again.

'Kelly Greenaway. I work at her club as a receptionist in the mornings. She lets me use her dance studio to practise in but she gets her pound of flesh in return. Right little tyrant she is, but Sean couldn't get enough of her. He was always pestering her to meet him. Anyway I heard them arrange to go for a drink that night in the pub. I guessed he would be there first because he seemed so – you know – eager.' Rosie paused to finish her drink. 'All I did was turn up at the Castaway early and I had a go at Sean, told him what had happened. He got quite nasty, told me to get lost and wouldn't give me any money.'

'Go on,' Macy said when Rosie came to a halt.

'Well, this is the bad bit.' She looked at him guiltily. 'While I was there, he had a phone call. He had to go to the bar to take it. I just put my hand in his jacket pocket. He had a hundred quid in his wallet. I took it. The shit deserved it,' Rosie concluded feelingly.

'And then you had to leave before he realized?'

Rosie nodded. 'While he was still on the phone,' she explained. 'I was shocked when you told me he was dead. I thought my jaw must have hit the table but you didn't seem to notice so I said nothing.'

'And you didn't tell the police?'

'They didn't ask me until this morning, funnily enough, when they came to the club. I didn't want them to know the whole story – it doesn't put me in a very good light, does it?' Rosie paused and added defensively, 'Anyway Kelly told me to act like Sean had never been near the place because she wanted to protect the good name of the club.' She sighed. 'Well, that's just about it really.'

'You told us you didn't work at Greenaways,' Macy pointed out.

'Yes, I did, didn't I?' Rosie said airily. 'I was shit-scared, to be honest. You come up and tell me Sean's dead: it's a wonder I didn't have a heart attack. My first thought was to have as little to do with it as possible so I denied all knowledge.'

Macy touched her arm. 'Thanks for telling me all this.

I'll try not to tell anyone else. I might go and see your boss, though – will she be at the club?'

Rosie took Macy's wrist in order to see his watch. 'No. It closes early tonight. She'll probably be at home, which is just round the corner.' She told Macy the address as they walked back across the car park. 'What do you want to see Kelly for?'

Macy was saved an explanation by Dean's reappearance in the doorway, telling Rosie to hurry up and get changed because the minibus was waiting. She swore back and said to Macy, 'He's a right little bully, isn't he? I've got a nose for them.'

Chapter Twenty-One

Before she could meet Kelly Greenaway, Jo had to collect her notes from the flat. Weaving through the rush-hour traffic on to the ring-road, Jo was annoyed with herself, not only for leaving so little time to get to Kelly's but also for not bringing the notes with her.

She could have done without the added stress of being late because Kelly had proved to be a difficult subject to study. Jo had been right in thinking that her chart would be interesting: she was a typical cool-headed Aquarian in some ways, unconventional and quick thinking and with a good business sense, as Jo had expected. But most Aquarians Jo had met were interested in people – they usually embraced many weird friends and causes – whereas Kelly was self-absorbed. Her Ascendant and a cluster of planets in Aries made her egocentric and tough – even reckless. There was no doubt about her ambition, either – Jo guessed she could be quite ruthless. With Capricorn at the Midheaven, Kelly was aspirational and a social climber and this went along with indications of a deprived or difficult childhood. Jo had been working on a tactful way of putting over some of these unflattering characteristics, knowing Kelly was too shrewd to be easily deceived. She also had the onerous task of pointing out that the immediate future looked fraught. It wasn't going to be a particularly easy consultation.

To increase her blood pressure further, all the traffic lights on the way to Earlsdon were against her and what she thought was a short cut beside Spencer Park turned out to be blocked by roadworks. While waiting at another red light, she decided that the first thing she would do when she got home would be to ring Kelly to apologize for being late.

She parked the car at the kerb and raced indoors, grabbing the post from her letter box and taking the stairs two at a time. While she waited for Kelly to answer the phone, she threw her mail on the table and found the folder she had prepared. She deposited her work for the astrology column on top of the computer. She had managed to finish it and it now only needed typing up ready to be delivered tomorrow.

Kelly was very pleasant on the phone, saying that she had only just got her daughter to bed anyway so it didn't matter if she was a bit late. Jo said she would set off straight away and should be there in a quarter of an hour. As she was speaking, one of the letters she had brought in caught her attention. She picked it up as she absently said goodbye to Kelly. The envelope was hand-written in ink and it had the heavy feel of expensive paper. The post mark was London SW15. Jo ran her thumb along the top and took out a single piece of notepaper and a cheque.

Dear Jo,

What do they say about heat and kitchens? Anyway I'm going to Dublin for a while. This serves the purpose of getting me out of the way while I try to borrow the money to pay off Sean's debtors. I'm hoping that you and Macy find a way of getting the buggers locked up but I will pay them if it comes to it. I enclose a cheque so you can carry on the work and I can be reached at the Dublin PO Box address above if you have any news. Better still, write to say you're coming to see me. I'll let my family know where I am. Don't think too unkindly of me,
Connor.

Inexplicably, she felt her throat tighten after she had read the last line. She looked at the cheque to distract herself. It was made payable to Macy and Wilson and was reasonably generous. She knew she would not be going to Dublin but she couldn't help a sneaking liking for Connor.

Before she set out to see Kelly, she rang Macy. Celia had gone home and there was only the answering machine so she left a succinct message saying she had heard from Connor. She supposed Macy would write to him, explaining Nick's involvement and death – and about the burglary. Connor could presumably come back if the police found Sean's drug suppliers or if they thought he would be safe.

Kelly did not live far from the club and Jo parked in a wide, quiet road. The houses were set back behind a line of trees so it was difficult to see the numbers. She stepped out on to the grass verge and walked along, peering up drives until she came to number 118.

It was a substantial detached house, built in the 1930s, Jo guessed, in a solid, appealing style with lots of small windows and a roof which swept down to cover the porch. It was the kind of house Jo imagined living in when she indulged in a mental fantasy about being happily married with a brood of kids. Thank God it was just a fantasy, she thought, as she pressed the doorbell.

Kelly's husband opened the door. He was a tall, burly man with a florid complexion and a not unhandsome face. He looked older than Kelly – in his forties, Jo guessed. He made rather strained small-talk as he showed her into a large room at the front of the house, where Kelly was watching television. Sitting on the huge sofa, with her legs tucked neatly under her, she looked even more diminutive than Jo remembered.

'Hello at last. I've been looking forward to this evening.' Kelly smiled up at her. 'Fancy making me wait – I would have thought you astrologers could foresee problems so you never got delayed.'

Jo apologized again but Kelly didn't seem to listen. 'You two haven't met, have you?' she said before Jo had finished speaking. 'This is my husband, Mark.' She stood up, putting her arm round his waist, which drew attention to the contrast between her neat, blonde figure and his dark, large one.

'I've got some coffee ready, could you make it for us?' She looked up at Mark. 'I thought Jo and I would go into the morning-room. You'll be able to watch the television then, won't you?' Kelly's voice descended into baby talk when she addressed her husband, Jo noticed disapprovingly. But he just smiled at her fondly and went off to make the coffee while Kelly led the way into a little room on the opposite side of the hall. Jo, who was only slightly taller than average, felt large and ungainly following behind Kelly's compact figure, which was clad in an expensive-looking jogging suit.

Jo settled down beside Kelly at the polished gate-leg table and took out her notes. She launched into her interpretation, highlighting Kelly's positive points like her organizational skills, her courage and resourcefulness. Jo's own enthusiasm for the subject came through and Kelly was a good listener. Jo drank two cups of coffee from a cafetière supplied by Mark and she was so engrossed that she hardly noticed how good it was.

They were coming to the end when they were interrupted by a child's crying from upstairs. Kelly looked up but before she could move, Mark popped his head round the door to say he would go to see what was wrong. Kelly turned to Jo, relieved. 'Poor Nina. She still gets nightmares after her ordeal earlier this year.'

'I remember hearing about it on the news,' Jo said, putting her own notes together and passing the presentation folder to Kelly. 'You must have been worried to death.'

'I was,' Kelly said fervently, 'I even made an appeal on television, I was so desperate. I never really thought we would get her back.' She paused, her face tight with the memory, and then she looked back at Jo and seemed to gather herself again. 'Thank you for this work. I'm very pleased – you've said all sorts of things about me which I recognize. Now, I've had your jacket mended and it's as good as new. It's at the club. Do you fancy a walk over there to get it?'

Jo agreed. The little room was stuffy and the idea of a walk appealed. Kelly went upstairs to tell Mark where they were going and came down carrying a rolled towel under her arm. 'He's reading her stories,' Kelly smiled as she opened the front door. 'I told him I was going for a swim. I often go over in the evenings when the club's closed. It's the only time I get to use the facilities myself. Have you thought any more about joining?'

'Oh, I don't think I can afford it,' Jo said honestly. She had almost forgotten that she had said she wanted to be a member when she had been snooping around the place but Kelly accepted her answer philosophically and they walked on in silence for a while.

'It's funny, but do you remember the chap who gave you the recommendation to this place?' Kelly said as they walked up the steps to the club. 'Sean Fitzpatrick, wasn't it? The police were here today asking about him – if I knew him, if he was a member and so on. Have they been to see you?'

'Not exactly. I've been to see them.' Jo decided she might as well admit her involvement. While Kelly let them in and led her into the kitchen, she explained that she had been working for Sean Fitzpatrick's brother. Kelly seemed to be only half-listening. She found the jacket and handed it over while Jo was talking.

'Tell you what,' she said when Jo had paused for breath, 'why don't you come for a swim, I remember you said you liked swimming. I've got a spare costume. You won't get a chance to use an empty pool like ours very often—?'

Jo looked up from examining her jacket, which seemed

as good as new. Although it was early in the evening, she felt strangely tired. But Kelly was insistent and Jo eventually agreed. It seemed an odd idea but it had been a hot day and a few lengths in the luxury pool might be quite pleasant.

'I'll go and get a costume,' Kelly said, looking pleased. 'See you down at the pool.'

Kelly went off cheerfully and Jo, smothering a yawn, made her way to the basement. She remembered the way down the dim flight of stairs to the pool. There was just enough light from the windows above not to need a light on. She hesitated at the bottom, wondering which set of double doors led to the pool and in that second she heard a noise, like a murmur or a stifled laugh but strangely echoing. As it seemed to come from ahead of her, Jo didn't see how it could be Kelly.

She pushed the door nearest to the direction of the noise and heard it again. It sounded like someone groaning this time. As she opened the door, the pool lay dark and undisturbed in front of her. What she could see of the tiled room looked tidy and empty; the whirlpool bath was still. Jo wondered where to find a light switch. She heard a gasp and a scuffle. She suddenly knew there was someone else there in the room and her mouth went dry.

She didn't call out. But she knew whoever was there must have heard her come in. She was moving along beside the wall, feeling desperately for a light switch. All she could feel beneath her fingers were smooth tiles. Not far in front of her, she thought she saw some movement but she couldn't work out what. Then her hand found a switch.

In an instant the place was lit up, yellow light bouncing off blue water. Jo was staring straight ahead at a couple on the floor, lying in an embrace and frozen with anxiety. Then a woman disentangled herself and sat up, meeting Jo's eyes with a rueful expression and struggling back into her swimming costume, which she was only half wearing, 'Who on earth are you?' she asked warily. Her partner raised herself on one elbow and looked up at Jo nervously through untidy long hair.

Sudden relief that she was not under any threat made Jo speechless for a second but in that time she remembered who the first woman was. It was Jane, who had been at the reception desk when Jo had first tried to get in the club. 'I'm with Kelly,' Jo said quietly. 'What are you doing here? I thought this place was closed.'

'Don't tell Kelly, will you, for God's sake?' Jane said. 'She'd definitely sack me.'

'She'll be here any minute,' Jo warned.

Both women were now on their feet and scrambling into towelling wraps. 'There's a way out this way,' Jane said, grabbing her partner's hand and heading to the back of the pool. The other woman, whom Jo did not recognize, remained quiet throughout, following Jane without question. 'Please don't say anything, will you?' Jane pleaded as they hurried past in bare feet. 'We don't do this very often but Kelly doesn't normally come down here at nights.'

'Of course,' Jo said vaguely, feeling faintly bemused. The two women hurried out past the locker room and Jo found a bench to sit on. Whether it was the shock of disturbing the women or simply her late night last night, she felt very tired and detached. She wondered if she was coming down with flu and something else bothered her: Jane had said Kelly didn't usually go down to the pool but Kelly had said she often went swimming at night.

She was still sitting there puzzling this out when Kelly arrived carrying a towel and swim suit. 'You're about a size ten, aren't you?' Kelly asked. She didn't say what had delayed her and Jo realized that was probably because nothing had. Jane and her partner had only taken seconds to leave.

Jo felt less like the idea of swimming now but she

didn't have the energy to argue with Kelly. She went to the locker rooms and put on her costume, leaving her clothes neatly folded on a bench. Kelly was already in the water when Jo came out. The lights seemed so bright after the locker room that her eyes hurt. She was consumed with a desire to lie down and go to sleep and suddenly decided it would not be a good idea to swim when she felt like this. She had better go home and go to bed, she thought.

'I'm going to give it a miss,' she called to Kelly, 'I'm not feeling too good. I'll let myself out, don't worry.' She turned back to the locker room but Kelly hauled herself out of the pool and came up to her. Kelly's face, dripping with water, looked up at her worriedly. 'What's wrong? Can I get you anything?'

'No, nothing,' Jo smiled, 'I just feel I might be coming down with something, that's all—'

Kelly put a hand on her arm. 'Are you sure? Let's see if you've got a temperature.' She put her other hand up to Jo's forehead in an almost maternal gesture. Jo submitted to this concern reluctantly, longing to be home and horizontal. Then she felt the grip on her arm tighten. She stepped back involuntarily and Kelly's other hand grabbed an ample amount of her hair.

Jo's scalp felt like it was parting from her head. She let out an involuntary yell. Before she could struggle, Kelly shoved her violently at the pool. Her footing went, she grabbed at thin air, made contact with Kelly's shoulder and fell, bringing Kelly on top of her. They hit the water with a crash that hurt. Then Jo went under.

She saw the bottom of the pool and felt Kelly's hands grabbing at her, catching hold of her legs. She broke the surface, thrashing her arms and trying to get her breath. Her shocked and bemused brain remembered that Jane and partner couldn't be all that far away so she opened her mouth and her lungs and forced a scream out of her throat. She felt the wrench of it all through her body.

She opened her mouth again and Kelly ducked her. This time she swallowed water. She could feel the strong fingers pressing on the top of her head while she writhed to get away.

Random thoughts came to her while the pressure of water pounded her head: This is how Kelly killed Nick. That was the funny smell in his car: chlorine. She's going to kill me too. One of her kicks caught Kelly in the stomach and the hands came off her head for a moment. Jo struggled upwards.

The world above the water seemed to be tilting from side to side dangerously but Jo made out the side of the pool and headed for it. Jo was a reasonable swimmer but Kelly was a better one and began to catch her up. There was no bar along the side of the pool; in fact not much to hold on to at all, just a lip in the floor tiles, and Jo reached for that. One hand made contact with the grainy wet tiles, one shoulder was out. She yelled again at the top of her voice and felt Kelly's hands catch her legs.

'It's no good,' Jo gasped while her mouth was temporarily out of the water, 'I'm sending for your wedding pictures. Everyone'll see them—' Jo felt Kelly let go and made another lunge, hoping to pull herself out.

But Kelly had only gone back a little way. Jo turned her head to see the other woman launch herself at her. The seemingly hairless face and staring eyes hovered above Jo for a second and then Kelly's full weight drove her down. Jo could see nothing but water and felt the pressure of Kelly's thumbs on her throat, squeezing so breath wouldn't come.

Chapter Twenty-Two

Piercing lights swayed above her eyes. She could hear nothing at all. Then blackness. Then the lights again, shifting high up, and cold water lapping her face. From somewhere her mind produced the thought that she was floating. That meant she could turn over and start swimming. Still deaf and dazed, Jo tried this and the side of the pool came into view – but miles away. One stroke and then another. Arms heavy, white tiles in front, wavering and reappearing like wavy lines in her head.

She touched them. Cold, certain. She raised an arm to try to haul herself out but someone grabbed it. She tried to pull away, failed and blacked out again. When she opened her eyes, Jane's concerned face was hovering over her. The pain in her chest seemed to pin her to the tiled floor and the pounding was back in her head. Jo retched and water spurted out of her mouth. Jane's face went away. Someone was making a disgusting gurgling noise and someone else was speaking. She heard Macy's voice: soft and low-pitched. But she must be imagining that, her brain told her. A woman said she had phoned an ambulance.

'I'm not going to hospital,' Jo muttered, 'I've got a phobia about hospitals.' She meant this to be an amusing remark but it came out as an incoherent noise. Jane's face reappeared and Jo recognized her Australian accent but couldn't distinguish the words.

She was aware of the stretcher and throwing up more

water and the ambulance. The motion was horrible. This time the ceiling really was moving about, Jo reassured herself, and she could hear Macy again but couldn't see him.

When she woke up properly he was definitely there. The walls around her were so bare that it could only be a hospital. There were screens in one corner and blinds at the window. Macy was standing with his back to her. He seemed to be peering through the blinds. She lay for a while and watched him and noticed that the pain in her chest seemed to have moved up to her throat and it hurt to move anything.

Jo was so glad to see him that it made her irritable. 'What are you doing here?' she tried to say and was pleased to notice that the words came out correctly, even though her voice was unrecognizable.

Macy turned round. 'I'm staying out of the way of the police. Alan's speaking to them, relating our successes. It's his big moment,' he said amiably. 'How are you feeling?' He came over and stood looking down at her.

'Terrible. Where am I?' Jo croaked.

'In a recovery room at the Walsgrave. I asked for you to be allowed to stay on your own, seeing as you've got a phobia about hospitals.'

This forced a grin out of Jo but it was disturbing to discover that anything but very shallow breathing hurt her chest. Her throat didn't want her to speak but she had some information to impart so she made an effort.

'Kelly was Sean's wife,' she said. 'It came to me when she threw me in the pool.'

'A brilliant piece of deduction,' Macy said, sounding quite cheerful.

'What happened?' Jo asked. Her mind was trying to put together a logical sequence of events after she was thrown into the pool.

'Unfortunately Rosie waited until after you left before letting out the crucial information: that it was Kelly Sean was coming to see. So I called the police, knowing you were there. Then I extravagantly caught a taxi and beat them to it because they went to her house and we went to the club. Oh, I asked Alan to meet me there too. Safety in numbers,' he added sheepishly.

'And there was I being half drowned.' Jo swallowed painfully. 'I'm sure she gave me a sedative or something in that coffee she made. I noticed she didn't have any—'

'Do you want a drink? There's some water here.' He poured her out a glass, while Jo shifted gently into a more upright position. She took the glass with stiff fingers and drank. 'Alan and I rushed to your rescue,' Macy went on, 'but that big Australian girl was seeing to you so we went upstairs and found Kelly stuffing money into a sports bag. Planning another flit, I think.'

'You spoke to her?'

'Only briefly until the police turned up.' Macy sat on the edge of the bed. 'Inspector Merson told me she hadn't even got a divorce from Sean.'

'She's a bigamist?' Jo's sore throat forced her to be succinct.

'Yes. Not a law which is often enforced but she had never told anyone about her other life and Sean could have wrecked everything for her just by showing up.'

'Blackmail?' Jo croaked.

'Sean was the kind of person who could never have enough money. He kept on asking Kelly and she kept on paying him off.' Macy paused and poured some more water for Jo. 'I'm hypothesizing of course.'

Jo wished she was in full voice and could sarcastically remind him that he was always criticizing her hypotheses. Instead she took a long drink and concentrated her energies on what she knew of Sean and Kelly. 'He was a pig to her when they were married – physical abuse as well.' Since she had learned that Sean and Kelly were married, she had been mentally comparing their charts and coming up with a clearer picture of them both. Kelly had mentioned during their consultation that both her parents had died when she was young and she was brought up in a foster family. She must have married Sean when she was very young and been dependent on him. It would be in character for Sean to abuse this power. But when the worm finally turned, Kelly's isolation would make it easier for her to drop out of one life and start another.

It was beyond Jo to put this into words just then and Macy, whose mind was obviously running along the same lines, was saying, 'She must have made a new identity for herself when she walked out on him – but he caught up with her again somehow.'

'On the telly,' Jo said. 'She made an appeal when her little girl went missing.'

She saw Macy raise his eyebrows appreciatively. 'Possibly. Anyway Nick must also have known about her. Sean may even have told him,' he reflected.

'It figures – Cass said he was always boasting about—' Jo stopped to swallow with difficulty.

'His various scams?' Macy supplied. 'Yes, I can imagine that. He must have thought he could trust Nick as they were both in the shit together at work. But Sean underestimated how badly Nick wanted out of that mess. Nick didn't want his job going down the pan, whereas I don't think Sean cared.'

'Kelly was the ideal ally for Nick. They both wanted to get rid of Sean.' Jo took another gulp of water. 'Somehow he traced her and they arranged to kill Sean between them. I knew he must have had an accomplice.' She sank back on the pillow in satisfaction.

Macy stretched out his arms and studied the ceiling. 'It wouldn't have been that difficult to find Kelly,' he mused, 'Nick only had to follow Sean on one of his trips to the Midlands. Then he must have talked her into helping him get rid of Sean.'

'Maybe Kelly didn't need a lot of persuasion.'

Macy made an agreeing noise. 'She bought the car well

in advance and went to meet Sean in it a few times so he got used to seeing her in it; chose the location – near the sailing club, which she belongs to – set Sean up with a call saying her car had broken down. She was at the club then, highly visible behind the reception desk. She lent Nick the clothes so he would look like her from the back. He's not that tall and it was dusk. Sean was expecting to see Kelly and was used to the car. But that distinctive red and white jacket proved to be a pain.'

'Why didn't Nick throw it away?'

'God knows. Kelly said they had agreed not to see each other again but Nick didn't stick to that. He kept ringing her up and asking to see her. It was like he got off on the idea of their being conspirators. She said she had to see him because Mark was making a fuss about the jacket. It was an expensive one and he'd bought it for her. So she had to see Nick again just to get it back. She just decided he was too unreliable and she would be better off with him out of the way.'

'So she drowned him in the pool.' Jo sighed. 'And tried to repeat the episode with me.'

'The difference was Nick was pretty drunk, according to the police,' Macy said, 'so he probably didn't put up much of a fight. It wasn't a bad plan. Merson – you know, the police inspector – he told me it's very difficult to tell if someone had died by drowning. And if he's fully clothed and bone dry, it's not something they'd be looking for. She was going to dump him in the reservoir I suppose but those kids put her off. She had a bike in the back of the car and just left him and cycled home.'

'We passed her,' Jo murmured. She was feeling battered but surprisingly better now that she had engaged her brain again. 'Sean made the classic mistake which Taureans can make: he let money rule his life. And he miscalculated about Nick. Never under-estimate a Scorpio.'

'I'll remember that,' Macy said sarcastically, unable to

maintain his bedside manner for long. 'The stars didn't lead you to Kelly, did they? You thought Rosie was Nick's accomplice.'

'If I'd had an inkling there was a connection between Sean and Kelly, I'd have been looking for the right things.'

'You've always got a good excuse,' Macy countered. 'Anyway, you're very talkative for someone who's been half strangled. What have you got to be so cheerful about?'

'I just remembered. I know where Connor is so I can bill him for Sean's chart. And Kelly wrote me a cheque before I left the house.'

'She probably felt safe you wouldn't be around to cash it,' Macy grinned appreciatively.

'True.' Jo gave a painful laugh. 'I was hoping she would recommend me to other people but I don't think she'll be moving in the same social circles now.'

'Maybe she'll tell Inspector Merson about you?' Macy suggested idly.

'No good,' Jo croaked, 'he's a sceptical Capricorn. But I'll still get my best month's earnings for a while. And there's money coming from you—'

'All right,' Macy interrupted irritably, 'you know I'll pay you. What were you saying about Taureans taking money too seriously?'

'I don't have to worry. I'm a Virgo. Just looking after the important details as usual.' Jo relaxed back on her pillow and smiled at him smugly. Her head ached and when she swallowed it felt as though someone was standing on her neck but despite this discomfort a feeling of satisfaction settled over her. She had told Connor she would find out what happened to Sean and she had.